A CANDLELIGHT INTRIGUE

CANDLELIGHT INTRIGUES

- 500 THE GOLDEN LURE, Jean Davison
- 504 CAMERON'S LANDING, Anne Stuart
- 506 THE WIDOW'S ESCORT, Beth De Bilio
- 508 WEB OF DECEPTION, Francesca Chimenti
- 510 PEREGRINE HOUSE, Janis Flores
- 514 THE PHANTOM REFLECTION, Ann Ashton
- 518 THE HAUNTING OF SARA LESSINGHAM, Margaret James
- 520 PERILOUS HOMECOMING, Genevieve Slear
- 523 DEMONWOOD, Anne Stuart
- 524 TEARS IN PARADISE, Jane Blackmore
- 528 THE COACHMAN'S DAUGHTER, Jane Creekmore
- 529 IMAGE OF EVIL, Rosemary A. Crawford
- 533 VILLE-MARIE, Bernice Wolf
- 534 THE GHOST OF LUDLOW FAIR, Evan Heyman
- 538 GRAVETIDE, Carolyn McKnight
- 539 DRAGONSEEDS, Barbara Banks
- 543 RING THE BELL SOFTLY, Margaret James
- 544 GUARDIAN OF INNOCENCE, Judy Boynton
- 550 HOME TO THE HIGHLANDS, Jessica Eliot
- 551 DARK LEGACY, Candace Connell
- 556 WHERE SHADOWS LINGER, Janis Susan May
- 557 THE DEMON COUNT, Anne Stuart

The Demon Count's Daughter

ANNE STUART

A CANDLELIGHT INTRIGUE

Published by
Dell Publishing Co., Inc.
1 Dag Hammarskjold Plaza
New York, New York 10017

Copyright © 1980 by Anne Kristine Stuart Ohlrogge

All rights reserved. No part of this book may be
reproduced or transmitted in any form or by any
means, electronic or mechanical, including photocopying,
recording or by any information storage
and retrieval system, without the written permission
of the Publisher, except where permitted by law.

Dell ® TM 681510, Dell Publishing Co., Inc.

ISBN: 0-440-11907-3

Printed in the United States of America

First printing—April 1980

With love, for Uncle A.

CHAPTER ONE

It took me most of the evening to pack. My supposedly vanished impulsiveness stood me in good stead as I went through my wardrobe with ruthless abandon, choosing the dullest, plainest clothing I owned. I debated for a full minute over the moderate hoop that was de rigueur for a fashionable young English girl in 1864, remembering at last my modern, collapsible model, which would just fit into my one large carpetbag. I doubted I could manage to carry more than that on horseback, and horseback seemed the only way I could escape to the coast without dear Uncle Mark alerting the countryside. I had every intention of writing him a polite note, explaining it was my patriotic duty to follow my other godfather's quixotic suggestion and make straight for Venice, the city of my father's birth. The trip would take me no more than a week, I estimated, and by the time I reached Venice, Bones would have convinced Uncle Mark there was nothing to worry about, at the same time dispatching his guardian angel to see that I came to no harm.

I stared across the room to the full-length mirror, the wavering candlelight giving my flamboyant looks a warm, melting sheen they usually lacked. It was fortunate that Bones had started the whole thing by suggesting I travel to strife-torn Italy. I would have an extremely difficult time trying to sneak there in disguise. There are very few women of my proportions wandering around Europe.

I could have wished my resemblance to my beloved parents a little less pronounced. From my father I inherited raven black hair that was thick and unruly and always managed to escape even the most severe pinnings. My eyes were golden like his, but undeniably warmer with what I have been told is a sweetness of expression to equal my mother's. I had her retroussé nose, rather than father's beak, and her full, red lips. If I hadn't been cursed with such an extraordinary body, I would have been quite pretty.

But there fate and family resemblance had let me down. From my father I had been bequeathed a generosity of height that left me towering over every man I had ever met, with the exception of my father, my older brother, and a few very foppish young men I had met last year in London.

From my mother I had inherited curves so voluptuous as to be downright embarrassing. As the years passed and I began to ripen, I sought desperately to try to tone down my overly feminine attributes. But all the running, jumping, climbing, and horseback riding only served to develop me more fully, so that I had become sadly accustomed to the wide-eyed astonishment my first appearance elicited. Men's eyes usually glazed over when introduced. Looking up into my eyes, their second reaction was either a stiff invitation to dance or a quick tussle in the garden. It was no wonder I had barely lasted a month in my disaster of a season. It was my own secret sorrow that I had longed for some man of a different sort to carry me away from all that superficial glitter. But such a man didn't seem to exist. At least I hadn't met him in twenty-three years.

All in all I was hardly the type to blend into a background, and I could only hope I would be able to accomplish Bones's mission while appearing to be a simpering tourist. If not, well, I needed an adventure, and a trip to Venice and the long-deserted family palazzo would be adventure enough in itself, even if it failed to include midnight meetings and secret information.

I paused momentarily in my hasty packing and

thought back to Lord Bateman's startling proposition this afternoon.

"I need you to go to Venice," Bones had announced with his usual startling abruptness, the china teacup trembling only faintly in his aged, cadaverous hands. "There's no one else, or you know I wouldn't ask, who's so admirably suited for the job. Your parents aren't around to hold you back, and you're just wasting your time moping around. It's time you did something."

"I'm willing, Bones," I answered mildly enough, accustomed to my godfather's excitability and impulsiveness. "To what job am I admirably suited?"

He barely hesitated. "My dear Luciana, I shouldn't ask it of you. But I do ask it, because I know you and trust you. The political climate of Europe right now is like a tinderbox. Austria is just about ready to hand Venice over to France in exchange for various political amenities. My sources also tell me that once that happens it's only a matter of time before Napoleon III cedes it back to Italy."

"But that's splendid!" I breathed, eyes aglow.

"Yes, and no. It is indeed splendid if all works out," he harrumphed. "Unfortunately, there have been a few obstacles thrown in the path of independence for La Serenissima. That's where I need your help.

"The powers that be in Venice do not fancy losing their somewhat tarnished jewel of a city. Therefore General Eisenhopf and Colonel von Wolfram have managed to obtain a certain very incriminating document. If that document were to be published, all our hopes would be dashed."

"What document?" I brushed the crumbs from my drab riding habit.

"A foolhardy document, fully authenticated, stating France's intention of attacking Austria once they have regained possession of Venice. Using that well-situated city and the Veneto as a base of operations. A stupid piece of business that Napoleon III rashly concocted a number of years ago, a plan he has no intention whatsoever of carrying out. But, needless to say, all Franz Josef needs is a hint of such a thing and years of careful diplomacy will have been wasted. Europe is about to explode; we must move very, very carefully."

"But why haven't these two Austrians produced this paper?"

"They are too busy bargaining. Neither Eisenhopf nor Von Wolfram have decided which they'd prefer: money or power. The price they're asking is far too high, anyway."

"But what can I do, Bones?" I cried. "Of what possible use could I be?"

Bones leaned back in his chair, a crafty smile playing around his withered lips. "Eisenhopf has one major weakness. And that is for women, particularly tall young women with abundant physical charms. In other words, someone like you."

"And you want me to seduce this old general into giving me the paper?" I jumped ahead, a little shaken.

Bones looked shocked. "Good God, no! You would never even come near the man. You will merely sneak into his room in the guise of a lady of the night while he's safely out of the city. And while you are there you'll retrieve the paper, hand it over to our informant, and return to England, secure in the knowledge that you have saved Venice."

"It sounds deceptively simple," I remarked, trying to control the fire of determination that was sweeping over me. "But how am I to manage all this? Gain admittance to his room, among other things?"

"All that will be taken care of. The general's valet is a very stubborn, pro-Austrian creature. Fortunately his brother-in-law is a different sort entirely. It was Tonetti himself who came up with the idea, approaching our best man with it. You'd be working with him, Luciana, though of course I'd have a guardian angel watching over you."

"And what makes you think we can trust this Tonetti?" I questioned warily.

"The best of all reasons. Money."

"But haven't you countless trained women who'd be better able to do the job?" I felt compelled to ask. Though I knew deep inside that I would strangle anyone who tried to go in my place.

"No doubt. But none of them are del Zaglias." He leaned forward and clutched my hand with the intensity of a fanatic. "Venice has suffered under the Austrian yoke for so long the people are becoming dull and sullen. Even the *dimostrazióne*, which has kept social intercourse and the upper classes out of Venice, has begun to lose momentum. You, my dear, would put new life into the movement." He sighed. "The beautiful daughter of one of Venice's bravest sons, returned to save that gallant, beleaguered city . . ." A grim smile lit his aged face. "What with your ancestry and the general's penchant for large and beautiful young ladies, we could scarcely do better."

A little flattery only added fuel to my eagerness, and there I was, five hours later, furtively packing my bags.

My beloved parents and six brothers were off in Scotland, leaving me in the care of various young and old retainers and the myopic supervision of my second godfather, the very correct, somewhat fumbling Mark Ferland. I hadn't needed Bones's warning not to tell Uncle Mark. I knew from long association that Bones's former agent looked back on all that derring-do with embarrassed dismay.

"Miss Luciana, what are you doing in there?" A querulous voice sounded at the door, and I thanked heaven I had had the foresight to lock it. Maggie had the sharpest eyes and the quickest tongue of anyone I had ever known, and ever since my mother had made her my personal maid and companion, nothing in my life remained private. I had no intention, however, of taking her to Edentide if I could help it. For one thing, her curiosity would be bound to interfere with my meetings with the mysterious and romantic-sounding Tonetti, and for another, she had a roving eye to equal the worst rakehell, and I had no doubt that the combination of her randiness and the Italian male would end in a brouhaha I could well do without. Besides, I was jealous.

"Not a thing, Maggie," I yawned convincingly. "I was tired from my ride over to Lord Bateman's and thought I'd get an early night's sleep." I bounced a few times on the bed for effect. "You may have the rest of the evening off," I added grandly.

"Oh, indeed?" Her voice was wry, and it was all I could do to remember that she was two years younger and a head shorter than me. "And why have you locked your door, tell me that?"

"Did I?" I murmured vaguely. "It must have been an accident. You know how these old doors are. Never you mind, Maggie. I'm too tired to get up and unlock it. I won't need anything more tonight. Why don't you go and visit Bitsy?"

"I have better things to do than spend my evenings with my mother," she replied pertly. "But I don't like the sound of you, Miss Luciana. You never tire so easily. Are you sure you're not coming down with something?"

I laughed with what I hoped was suitable heartiness. "I'm as strong as a horse, Maggie. It must have been too much sun."

"Very well, miss. I can't say as I wouldn't appreciate an evening off. That William has been at me something awful. . . ." Her voice trailed away as she wandered down the hall, and I breathed a sigh of relief. Maggie was much too sharp by half, and even if I hid all the evidence of my intended flight, I doubted I could deceive her eagle eye.

I slept fitfully that night, tossing and turning and wrapping my overlong limbs in the linen sheets so that I felt as if I were in my winding sheet. First light found me wide awake and thankfully alert. I had never needed more than a very few hours of sleep. Dressing quietly, I slipped out my door and down the deserted hallways on silent feet, smugly aware that Maggie had failed to hear me from her adjoining closet. Of course there was no guarantee that she had actually slept in her own bed that night. Chances were she hadn't.

But my luck held all the way out to the stables. The only servant awake and moving around was a young groom of no more than thirteen, who sleepily saddled my younger brother's mare, accepted my notes for Maggie and Uncle Mark, and watched me ride off into the brilliant dawn with an incurious yawn on his young face.

I made excellent time that first day despite my concern not to overtire poor old Marygold, my ancient, but stately, mare. When night fell my first concern was to see to her well-being, and I conscientiously provided her with a good crop of grass to eat. As for me, I did equally well with the remains of a loaf of bread and a huge chunk of cheese stolen from the kitchens on my way out of the house and slept the darkness away quite comfortably under a hedge with my serviceable brown wool cape wrapped snugly around me to protect me from the chill of an August night in England.

By the next afternoon we were in Bournemouth, both of us rather the worse for wear, but our spirits intact. Marygold, after having been relegated to a boring life as a child's palfrey, was enjoying her sights of the wide world, though I didn't doubt she would retire gratefully back to pasture once her adventure was over. Indeed, she greeted her stall that evening with a whinny of tired pleasure, settling in with a sigh.

As luck would have it the Channel packet wouldn't leave till the next morning, and there was nothing I could do but take a room at the cleanest-looking waterfront inn I could find. And it was there they found me, tucking into a massive meal of pheasant, lobster, ale, and greens.

"Ahem." A loud throat-clearing broke through my food-clouded reverie, and I looked up with a sinking feeling to meet the warm, stern blue eyes of my other godfather, Mark Ferland. Standing by his side, her pert face set in an abnormally grim expression of profound disapproval, was Maggie.

I swallowed, once, twice, determined to regain my aplomb. I smiled up sweetly as the pheasant made its way down my throat and signaled the waiter for more plates. "Uncle Mark! Maggie! What a lovely surprise! Are you planning to accompany me to Venice?"

My bright innocence stopped Uncle Mark for a moment, but Maggie was undeterred. "No, we aren't, Miss Luciana, and well you know it. We've come to take you back to Somerset, and no more of your tricks."

I surveyed my maid for a moment, my mind working feverishly while, with my usual amazement, I took in her far from prepossessing appearance.

Maggie Johnston was a cheerfully well endowed girl of twenty-one with a pert little nose and a sharp tongue, copper curls twisted up on her small head, a rosy complexion flushed with annoyance. Her weakness for pretty clothes was apparent in the fanciness of her blue-sprigged traveling dress, and I knew half her irritation was for the dust on her elegant toilette. I smiled up at her beguilingly. Next to my mother and our ancient Maddelena, she was the woman I loved most in this world.

"Oh, for heaven's sake, sit down and stop glowering at me, Maggie," I exclaimed, pushing a chair out for her. "You, too, Uncle Mark. You're wrecking my appetite with your sour faces."

Maggie's glower abated only a trifle as she seated herself with ladylike grace. Uncle Mark, as usual, took his cue from the strongest personality present. His troubled blue eyes moved from Maggie back to me with vague concern.

"Now see here, Luciana," he began pompously, knowing full well how foolish he sounded. "As your godfather and the only man around who can stand in loco parentis, I must insist that you return with us immediately. When Bones told me you'd gone racing off I couldn't believe my ears. It's just not done, Luciana, my dear, and you know that as well as I do."

I leaned back and stared at them, a mutinous expression settling around my mouth.

"There is little that angers me, Uncle Mark, but the one thing I detest is being told what is and isn't done," I said in a desperate undertone. "It *is* done, because I have just done it. And if you intend to try to take me back home, you had best be prepared to use physical force. I won't leave without kicking and screaming and telling everyone you are white slavers bent on abducting me."

"Luciana!" Mark pleaded helplessly. "What would your father say?"

"He'd be very amused," I replied, not at all sure I was right. My father had a severe streak underneath his cynical lenience, a streak I had crossed, to my sorrow.

"We could always drug your wine, Miss Luciana," Maggie suggested pleasantly.

I grinned. "Are you sure you have no Italian blood, Maggie? I'm glad to be forewarned; I'll make sure I drink nothing that has passed your fair hands."

"For God's sake, Luciana, you can't be meaning to pursue this mad course!" Uncle Mark interrupted, running a harassed hand through his thinning brown hair. "Bones told me about your mission—it's not the child's play you seem to think. This man could be dangerous—there's no way you could be protected all the time. Isn't there some way we could dissuade you?"

There was, but neither of them was imaginative enough to threaten writing my father. The thought of his traveling to Venice to retrieve me would have put a swift end to Bones's wild scheme, but I counted on their knowing, if they had thought of such a possibility, that it would sign Luc del Zaglia's death warrant. The Imperial Army of Austria had a very long memory. "There is no way you could dissuade me," I said firmly. "You could always accompany me, of course."

I was fairly certain that Uncle Mark was Bones's hand-picked guardian angel, and I had little doubt he would succumb rather than let me go off on my own. Maggie was a question mark however.

My two pursuers shared a glance. Mark shrugged first. "It seems I have little choice, Luciana. As a gentleman and your godfather I could hardly watch you run off to that hotbed of espionage and insurrection without at least offering my protection."

I smiled my gratitude, breathing a sigh of relief. "And you, Maggie?"

She shrugged her plump shoulders in the stylish dress. "That William isn't half the man I'd hoped he'd be. Perhaps I might do better with a foreigner. Your father is a fine figure of a man, Miss Luciana. If any of them Eyetalians come close I'd be a happy woman."

"Take it from me, my girl," Uncle Mark said morosely, dwelling on ancient injuries, "there's no one like Luc del Zaglia." He refilled our wine glasses, then held up his glass in a toast. "To Venice, ladies! And let us pray I'm not making the worst mistake in a mistake-strewn life."

I lifted my glass, looking him squarely in the eye. "To Venice," I echoed. "To a free Venice and an end to Austrian tyranny!"

"To Venice," Maggie said dreamily, "and love."

I hesitated, but only for a moment. It was long past time to toss my bonnet over the windmill. I laughed aloud. "To Venice," I echoed, "and love."

CHAPTER TWO

The train began its way along the long Austrian-built causeway as we started on our last lap of the hurried, exhausting trip to the fabled city of Venice. I peered out through the soot-stained windows, eager for my first glimpse of the place that had meant more to me than the land of my birth, but in the late summer's twilight I could barely see the domed skyline in the distance.

"We're almost there." I turned to my companions. Maggie had her face pressed against the window while Uncle Mark nodded wearily and buried his nose once more in the paper. "Aren't you excited, Uncle Mark?" I demanded sternly. "We've finally reached our destination."

He put the paper down and sighed. "I must say I'm glad all our traveling is over. Though I'd be much happier if you saw reason and returned on the next train." He shook the paper into neat folds. "And no, I am not excited to be in Venice once more. My memories of the place are not my fondest."

"Why not? You met Mama there." I am a bit inquisitive, and at times almost lacking in tact.

"Because, Miss Busybody, I also met your dear father there, who proceeded to steal your mother away from me."

I had known all this for years, but never failed to be fascinated by it. "Pish, tush," I dismissed his complaints heartlessly. "Mama and Father were made for each other. You should have known that."

"Nevertheless," he announced with injured dignity, "I have never taken a bride."

I reached out and patted his hand, chagrined at my unsympathetic tone. "That is indeed a great shame, Uncle Mark, for all the women of the world." He cast a suspicious look at me out of his nearsighted eyes, but I spoke in all seriousness. "If it's any consolation to you, you've been my parents' best and dearest friend."

He sighed, a sound halfway between complacency and despair. "Yes, it's true," he said heavily. "It's probably just as well I never married. It wouldn't have been fair to give a lady only half a heart."

A small, strange noise came from Maggie, one I recognized as a snort, and I cast her a severe glance. I found my Uncle Mark's posturings as a heartbroken swain infinitely touching despite the fact he was, without a doubt, a born bachelor uncle.

"Best put your hat on, Miss Luciana," Maggie announced after an emotional pause. "And fix your hair. You do look a sight."

I rose and peered into the velvet-framed mirror the Austrian engineers had thoughtfully provided the first-class passengers on this most modern of railway cars. Black hair was straggling over my green-clad shoulders, my sooty lashes added to the circles around my large topaz eyes, and my narrow face was pale with fatigue. Incompetently, I stuffed my hair back into the loose coil I usually wore, pulled on my far-from-fashionable bonnet, and, as an afterthought, stuck my tongue out at both my reflection and my disapproving maid.

"I scarcely do you credit, Maggie," I noted, watching her as she stuffed filmy scarfs, French novels, and half-eaten chocolates into one of the bandboxes she had brought along.

She cast a disparaging glance over my attire and sighed gustily. "I've long ago given up on making a fashion plate of you, Miss Luciana. I'm waiting till you fall in love. *Then* you might take some interest in your appearance."

"You may have to wait awhile," I warned her, striding nervously around our small, private compartment as the train began pulling to a stop.

"I've waited long enough already," she said sternly, primping in the mirror. "If you'd only . . ."

"Oh, please, Maggie, don't scold," I begged, practically dancing with excitement. "I want this moment to be perfect."

She sighed again, and Uncle Mark smiled benevolently. "Well, missy, I believe we've arrived. Would you like to be the first one out? To get your view of the city alone?"

I leaned down and gave him an exuberant kiss. "You know me so well, Uncle Mark. Bless you."

With a shrieking of steam, grinding of gears, and clanking of metal, the great engine finally ended its seemingly endless journey. Within a few moments more our door was opened and the steps lowered. With my heart pounding beneath my stiff green traveling gown, I put my gloved hand on the sooty railing and stepped down onto Venetian soil for the first time in my life.

My first sight of Venice was as astounding as I had expected it to be, though the subject matter I focused on with my excellent eyesight was far from what I had anticipated. Watching me from halfway across the crowded, dimly lit station was the most extraordinary man I had ever seen.

He towered over the Italians around him, even topping most of the much taller Austrian soldiers that milled aimlessly about the station. His hair was dark gold and cut long in that style that looks natural rather than contrived. His nose was straight, his mouth beautifully formed, his expression unreadable at that distance. But I knew with a certainty he watched me as I watched him, as I looked into the most beautiful deep silver-blue eyes I had ever seen. Never had I seen a man more handsome, with the possible exception of my father. And then he turned slightly, and I saw the scar.

Cut into one side of his magnificent face, starting up in the hairline and ending just above his strong jaw, was a fine, white line, marring his perfect beauty, yet somehow enhancing it. That one terrible imperfection mocking his handsome face and turning it into something far beyond mere good looks. A gusty sigh escaped me.

" 'oos that, Miss Luciana?" Maggie cooed in my ear, her eyes bright at the sight of an attractive male.

I stifled the angry jealousy that swept over me. "Isn't he the most handsome man you have ever seen?" I whispered.

She looked at me in amazement. "No," she said bluntly. "He's not half bad, but I would hardly say *the* most handsome. In the top fifty, perhaps..." she allowed cautiously, peering at him.

Shaking my head, I closed my eyes and sighed. "*The* most handsome, Maggie. Without question."

"What's all this?" Uncle Mark demanded, climbing from the railway carriage and unceremoniously pushing Maggie out of the way. "What's going on with you two?"

"Miss Luciana's fallen in love," Maggie announced, and I kicked her.

"Uncle Mark, who is that man?" I questioned urgently. "He must be British . . . no other race could look quite so arrogant."

"Which man, m'dear?" he murmured, casting myopic eyes out over the crowd.

"Why, over there . . ." I looked again, and to my sorrow, which was all out of proportion for such a little thing, I found that he had disappeared. "He's gone," I said flatly.

Maggie looked up from nursing her wounded leg, and the look in her hazel eyes was sympathetic. "Don't you worry, miss. You'll see him again. If it's meant to be."

I shook my head nervously, as if to deny my reaction to myself and to her. "Why, whatever do you mean? I'm sure you're making a mountain out of a molehill. He was just a very handsome man, that's all. I would hardly be human not to notice."

"That's all well and good, miss. But you've

never noticed before." She held up a thin, work-worn hand to hold off my protest. "Never you mind. I'll say no more on the matter. Not now, leastways."

"Seen an attractive fellow, eh, Luciana?" Uncle Mark boomed, still a few minutes in the past. "Well, chances are you'll meet him soon enough. Society, that is, English society, moves in very close circles in these foreign cities. Bound to come across the fellow sooner or later. Unless he's entirely ineligible, that is."

"For God's sake!" I swore, desperate. "The two of you are practically marrying me off, and I've never even spoken to the man. I wish you would just . . ."

"Yes, Fräulein?" A guttural German voice spoke from behind me, and I whirled around nervously.

My first sight of the hated Austrian army was fairly prepossessing. The young man in front of me could scarcely have been much older than I. We were of the same height, yet somehow his cold blue eyes seemed to look down on me with a sneer I found distinctly irritating.

"The Fräulein has yet to go through customs," he said stiffly. "If you will be so kind . . ." He gestured to his left, and with dismay I saw a long line of my fellow passengers, their luggage pawed through, their faces set in angry expressions of rage and exhaustion. "We have been having a bit of trouble with a small band of insurgents," the man continued blandly, "making it necessary to search all visitors' luggage for contraband. I am sure the Fräulein will be more than happy to assist the Austrian army in their duty."

"Now see here, Captain!" Uncle Mark blustered, and I quickly shushed him. There was obviously no help for it. I gave him a polite nod accompanied by the merest trace of a smile. "Of course, Captain." I headed off in the direction of the disgruntled line, and once more his meaty hand came down on my silk-clad arm. I halted, looking pointedly at the offending member until he removed it.

"We have a special place for you, Fräulein del Zaglia," he said heavily, and at the mention of my name my backbone stiffened in alarm. "Your companions may join the others, but we are determined to give you a better-than-average welcome. It is not often one of the ancient Venetian families chooses to return to their water-drenched city. The Imperial Army is very interested in your reason for doing so and most concerned as to whether we can expect the joy of your father's presence before too long, eh?" He smiled, revealing so many white, shining teeth I was quite revolted.

"My father has no intention of returning to

Venice," I replied stiffly. "Not until its invaders have left."

My captor glowered, the meaty hand descending once more. Against my will I felt myself being forced toward a dark and sinister-looking doorway, and I bit back the temptation to scream for help. Screaming would do no good . . . the Austrians were in charge here. They would be far more likely to assist the brute by my side. And all poor Uncle Mark and Maggie could do was stare at us helplessly.

"Telfmann!" A voice broke through my red haze of anger, and the hand released me immediately.

"Sir!" He saluted smartly, and I followed his gaze.

The officer who had accosted us was somewhere near middle age. He could have been anywhere from forty to sixty, with closely cropped blond-gray hair, cold, cold blue eyes, and a hard, cruel expression on his handsome, slightly bovine face.

"You will leave Fräulein del Zaglia to me," he said softly, menacingly in German. Thanks to my educated mother, I could understand every word. "I gave you orders that she was to be brought to me with the minimum of fuss, and I see you struggling all over the station with her. You have been inept, Telfmann."

"But sir," he protested, "how was I to know she was a bad-tempered giantess?"

I snorted indelicately, and the cold blue eyes met mine for a brief moment. I was not reassured.

"The Fräulein, like her mother, obviously understands German. You may leave us, Telfmann. I will deal with you later."

The younger man left quickly, protesting angrily in a muttered undertone, as I turned to face his replacement.

Having let my guard slip momentarily, I was anxious to regain lost ground. I put out one small-boned hand and gave him my most enchanting smile, reserved for Austrian pigs. "If you knew my mother then you must be Holger von Wolfram!" I cried ingenuously. "Mother has told me all about you." And Bones, too, I added silently, recognizing him as my enemy.

There was no change in his hard expression. "No doubt," he replied caustically. "And your father also, hein?" He cast a questioning glance back at the curious figures of Maggie and Uncle Mark, and even from a distance I could see Maggie's instinctive preen. Holger von Wolfram was far from unattractive, and Maggie, English as she was, lacked my instinctive hatred for the Austrians.

"That is my maid and companion, Maggie

Johnston," I offered brightly. "She's accompanying me on my small version of the grand tour. I decided when I reached France that I simply couldn't return home without visiting the family seat in Venice." I gestured toward Uncle Mark's stooped figure. "And you remember my godfather, Mark Ferland?"

"I am acquainted with Mr. Ferland," he said dryly. "And that is your reason for being here, Fräulein? To visit your heritage?"

I let out a light trill of laughter. "But of course! Why else should I venture alone to such an insalubrious place? No doubt my parents would disapprove heartily, but I failed to notify them of my intentions." I smoothed my bottle-green skirt, peeking up at the soldier with what I hoped was demure charm. "I'm sure I'll receive a great scold when I return."

"Your parents do not know you are here?" he demanded, an expression of disgust crossing his stolid face. "Bah, you are just like your mother! No doubt"—and here he smiled evilly—"your father, when he hears what you have done, will come and fetch you home again?"

And how you'd like that, I thought. "Oh, no. I expect to be back long before he even finds out I've gone. And they'll trust Mr. Ferland to take good care of me should I be delayed."

"You expect your business to be concluded so quickly, then?"

"Business?" I echoed innocently, enjoying this verbal fencing. My mother, in her tales of Venice, had failed to mention how very acute the good colonel could be. "What do you mean?"

He smiled. "Why, your pilgrimage to your ancestral home, of course. What else could I possibly mean?" He cleared his throat loudly, and I jumped. "Though I must warn you, Fräulein, that Venice is a dangerous place for people here on less harmless . . . business." There was a slight emphasis on the last word, and I barely controlled a shiver of dismay.

"I have no intention of doing anything more dangerous than sightseeing," I replied brightly, hiding my uneasiness like a practiced spy. "Really, Colonel, you sound like something out of Byron . . . full of dark deeds. Do you think someone will stab me and drop me in the canal?"

He bowed over my hand with mock gallantry. "It could be arranged, Fräulein. If necessary. *Auf Wiedersehen.*"

It took me only a moment to recover from the threat. "Good-bye, Colonel. No doubt we will see you again before we go."

"Have no doubt of it, Fräulein."

"Are you all right, Luciana?" Uncle Mark demanded as I finally reached his side. "Who was that fellow?"

"Do you remember Holger von Wolfram, uncle?" I questioned, and was not at all reassured to see the ruddy color drain from his face.

"Couldn't likely forget him. He nearly murdered your father, Luciana. He's a dangerous man, through and through. I advise you to keep clear of him." He paused, a puzzled look on his distinguished face. "Can't understand why he's still in Venice. He always hated the place. When I knew him twenty-five years ago he seemed a man destined to rise to the heights of his profession. Could have gone anywhere. Very strange."

"Well, I thought he seemed very attractive," Maggie announced obstinately. "In a fierce, angry sort of way. He seemed quite taken with you, Miss Luciana. If you're not interested I might try my hand there. It might be a treat to have an older man for a change."

"If you dare," I said angrily, "even think about consorting with the enemy, Maggie Johnston, I will personally see that you are strangled and dropped in the Grand Canal. That was how the Council of Three used to get rid of their enemies, you know." I tugged uselessly at the ill-fitting jacket. I was still shaken from my unexpectedly sudden encounter, and surreptitiously I cast my eyes around the crowded train station. If Tonetti was there, I could not tell. I would simply have to wait for him to make himself known to me.

Maggie was about to answer pertly when she recognized the abstracted expression in my usually mild eyes. "I'm only funning, Miss Luciana. You wouldn't think I'd actually lower myself to waste my time on an Austrian, would you? I doubt I'll have time to get through the Venetians." She chuckled, and reluctantly I smiled.

"Let's go home. Let's change our clothes, have some tea, and get to bed."

"I'd love to, Miss Luciana," she replied. "But where would 'home' be?"

"Why, Edentide, of course," I replied.

CHAPTER THREE

At all events, we didn't arrive at Edentide until early the next afternoon. "Dash it, no one's been in the place in years, with the exception of a few old retainers at infrequent intervals," Uncle Mark protested as we glided down the moonlit Grand Canal. I watched the silvery water float by us almost in a trance, forgetting for a moment why I was here in the enchantment of the August night. Uncle Mark pulled at his sparse and graying mustache, determined to hold my attention. "The place should be infested with rats. Best wait until we can send a few people in there to clean it up."

"But I can't afford to wait," I said stubbornly, pulling myself out of my moon-clouded dreams with an effort. "The sooner I take up residence, the sooner this Tonetti can contact me and I can set about Bones's business. Maggie and I are perfectly capable of doing a hard day's work. We can scrub and clean enough rooms to live in in no time at all."

"I must say I don't like the sound of this Tonetti

fellow. Anyone who'd help land a lady in a compromising position can be no gentleman."

"Oh, I have no doubt he's not a gentleman," I said cheerfully. "I'm hoping he's a rake and bears a striking resemblance to the man I saw in the train station tonight."

"Von Wolfram?"

"No!" I shrieked.

"Telfmann?" Maggie questioned, but I could tell from the sly expression in her eyes she knew perfectly well who I meant.

"No," I repeated in a milder tone of voice. "But it doesn't matter what he looks like, as long as we're able to do what I came here for. And you're not to interfere, either of you," I added warningly, placing no reliance on their agreement.

"How can you expect me not to interfere?" he demanded irritably. "You're putting your head in a noose, and it's my unfortunate duty to protect you."

"You can protect me," I allowed him graciously, "but you can't interfere. Or I'll have you carted back to England by one of Bones's henchmen."

"You couldn't!" he harrumphed.

"Oh, yes, she could," Maggie informed him grimly, recognizing the determined expression on my face. "Best leave her to handle it as she thinks best. In the meantime we have more important problems to deal with."

"And what problems are those?" I demanded with real curiosity.

She sniffed at my disavowal of the obvious. "Why, to find out who that devastating fellow was, to meet him again, and to do something about your wretched wardrobe. *I* wouldn't be caught dead in things you wear."

Normally I ignored Maggie's constant complaints, but for some reason tonight they struck a responsive chord. Perhaps it was the mood of the magic city, the wide expanse of the Grand Canal stretching out around us. Perhaps I had just reached the age to be interested in men. Or perhaps it was that man.

"May I suggest," Uncle Mark interrupted dryly, having recovered his equilibrium, "that we continue this discussion later? And that in the meantime we have this villainous-looking gondolier head for the nearest hotel catering to *English* travelers and plan what we shall do next. I know" —he held up a restraining hand at my bubbling protest—"you want to go directly to Edentide. No doubt we shall pass it on the way. If you do insist on cleaning the old wreck yourself, I will do all I can to assist you. But after a week of traveling I think we all deserve a good night's sleep on clean linen in a rat-free bedroom. Do you not agree?"

"You promise to let us go to Edentide tomorrow?" I demanded suspiciously.

"I most solemnly swear," he pledged, holding up his right hand in a theatrical gesture.

"In that case, an *English* hotel," I mimicked him, "would be most welcome."

No sooner had I reached my small, clean, English bedroom than I fell into a long, exhausted sleep, which was only slightly troubled by dreams. Dreams of the mysterious and romantic Venetian spy, Tonetti, who bore a startling resemblance to the scarred Englishman.

It wasn't until midmorning that I awoke, sunlight streaming in my hotel windows. Still in a stupor of sleep, I stumbled to answer the incessant knocking at my door and in a daze received an armful of flowers from a smirking chambermaid.

By the time I tipped her and locked the door behind her inquisitive figure, I was wide awake. It took me only a moment to find the note amid the fragrant mimosa blossoms, only another few seconds to scan the scrawled and ill-spelled message.

"Sweet Goddess," it began, "I saw you last night and gave to you my heart. Only say I might dare to hope. A brief glimpse of you is all I crave. I will be at the Merceria this morning by the perfume stalls. One small glance is all I ask, my precious pigeon. I live only for that moment. Your devoted slave, Enrico Addonizio Valentino Tonetti."

The scent wafting from the paper assured me that my admirer had already spent far too much time by the perfume stalls. I hesitated for only a moment. I ordered a brief meal and gobbled it in two minutes flat. Then I wasted another half hour pawing through my meager wardrobe, looking in vain for something the slightest bit flattering. Everything was either a muddy brown or a dull, bottle green, four years out of date, and more suited to a governess than a del Zaglia. It was a little past ten when I hammered on Maggie's door, bursting into her room with an excited good morning.

She eyed me from beneath the covers, a sour expression on her face. "What time is it?" she muttered suspiciously.

"Incredibly late, my girl. Past ten!" I threw open the shutters and stared out at the canal below me, my nostrils taking in the strong reek of sea water and garbage as it floated by.

"Miss Luciana," Maggie began in a dangerous tone of voice, tossing back the light covers, "we didn't arrive in Venice until past nine last night.

We didn't reach our rooms at this bleedin' hotel until after midnight, and we've been traveling hell-bent for the past week, during which I've not had a decent night's sleep the entire time. And you have the bloody nerve to come bouncing in here when I've just begun to catch up on me beauty rest . . ."

"Botheration!" I dismissed her complaints cheerfully. "Just look out at this beautiful city and tell me that you want to sleep some more!"

With great dignity and bedclothes trailing, she stalked to the window, stuck her curl-papered head out, withdrew it, and stalked back to the bed. "Yes!" she said succinctly, sitting down with a plop.

"With all those so very handsome Venetian men wandering around down there? And me with shopping to do, and no one to come with me and help me deal with them all?" I questioned mournfully.

In a twinkling the bedclothes were on the floor, followed by Maggie's nightgown, curl papers, and chin strap. Another couple of minutes had her turned out in great style in a cherry-red striped gown, which made me appear the gangling servant, towering as I did behind her in my sober green dress.

"And what shopping have we to do?" she demanded, pulling her reticule over one heavy-boned wrist. Despite my length my bones were delicately shaped, preserving me from looking too much a freak, and every now and then I thanked providence for that small mercy.

"Cleaning supplies, food, etc. The Merceria should be the place for all that. And I thought..." I let it trail off in sudden embarrassment.

"Yes?" she demanded, casting a knowing eye at my blushes.

"I thought we ... we might visit a dressmaker. I've heard a great deal about the Venetian dressmakers," I excused it lamely.

"Absolutely not!" she said stoutly, striding out into the hallway. "We will buy some lengths of cloth, and I will make some dresses for you. These Eyetalians cannot be trusted when it comes to the dressing of an English lady."

"But I'm half Italian," I argued. "And besides, I thought you fancied the Venetian men."

"I do, indeed. But what's good enough for me doesn't come close to being good enough for you, Miss Luciana. We might buy you some Venetian lace," she allowed generously. "But you'll leave it to me to make it up."

Maggie, when she got the bit between her teeth, was not to be moved, and indeed, in this case, I was just as happy to let her have her way. Having an eye for clothes and limited means, she'd learned to take a natural talent for the needle and turn it into an art, making some of my mother's most elegant dresses, and I had only to exercise the mildest of restraints as we pored over the bolts and bolts of rich fabric.

"I absolutely won't wear pink," I said firmly, dismissing a pastel silk an eager merchant in the Merceria thrust forward for my maid's exacting eye. The scent stalls were not far away, and I scanned them eagerly, hoping to recognize my partner in crime. I turned back to Maggie after a moment none the wiser. "I need something more subdued." I shifted the huge bundle of soaps and rags that we'd bought earlier, trying to make my point.

"All your life you've worn subdued clothing, Miss Luciana, and where has it got you? It's time for something more daring. That's it!" She pounced on a length of deep rose, holding it aloft with a cry of triumph.

"That's still pink," I said mutinously, won over despite myself by the glowing shade of the silk. I couldn't control the eerie sensation that we were being watched, and once more I shifted our purchases, casting a searching eye over the assembled shoppers. There was no sign of any devoted admirer, no sign of anyone the least bit suspicious-looking. The bustling, crowded shopping area of Venice, with its rich smell of spices, ancient fish, and fresh flowers, was even thankfully void of the bright white-and-gold uniforms of the Austrian invaders. I shook myself nervously. Tonetti hadn't promised he'd contact me—he'd said he only wanted a glimpse. Well, I had the nasty feeling he was getting an eyeful.

"Perfect," Maggie breathed over the silk, ignoring my objections, which were halfhearted anyway. "With a deep flounce in the skirt, a small crinoline..." she sighed dreamily, "and lace around the necklace. You'll look a dream, Miss Luciana."

"I do hope so," I said cynically, dropping soap on my foot. "Not that it matters."

"Of course it matters," she said stoutly. "And don't think I don't know what prompted this sudden interest in clothes. I'll tell you what: Each time you see your mysterious gentleman, I'll make you a new dress. That way you could get yourself a husband and a new wardrobe at the same time, the one helping the other, so to speak."

The rest of the soap followed onto the cobblestones, accompanied by packets of tea, sugar, ginger biscuits, and nectarines. "You'd best pick out some more material, Maggie," I said in a strangled voice. "He's over there." At the sight of the Englishman, Tonetti fled my mind completely.

She whirled around, nearly dropping the lovely rose silk into the mud along with our food. "Where?" she demanded.

"Stop staring," I hissed. "I don't want him to see us." He was quite a way up the alley, his back to us, the dark blond hair glinting in the sunlight that played cruelly on his scarred cheek. Maggie followed the direction of my gaze, sighing soulfully.

"I do think that scar is ever so romantic," she breathed. Turning briskly back to the eager vender, she pointed toward a bolt of deep blue cotton with tiny white flowers. "We'll take that, too." I turned around to protest, but she merely met my objections with a bland smile. "A bargain is a bargain, Miss Luciana."

My once-bulging reticule was sadly depleted at the end of our bartering. Out of the corner of my eye I had watched the tall Englishman, covertly fascinated by the long, lean strength of him. He seemed to have no particular business in the Merceria, merely wandering from stall to stall, paying no marked attention to anyone or thing. Not even, unfortunately, to me. For a moment I toyed with the idea that he was, in fact, Tonetti, and then reluctantly dismissed it. I had Bones's assurance that Tonetti was Venetian, and the man ahead of me was most definitely British. That, combined with his total lack of interest in me, forced me to abandon the romantic hope that he was my confederate. Turning to Maggie I suggested in an offhand whisper, "Why don't we just . . . sort of wander around and look at things?"

She grinned up at me. "I'm game if you are, Miss Luciana. Wouldn't want to let a live one get away." She trotted pertly off in his direction, leaving me to struggle behind, still clutching my myriad of parcels, desperate to stop my impulsive maid before she made a spectacle of the both of us. As we neared the Englishman she suddenly disappeared down a side lane beside a fish stall.

Rushing after her, I took no notice of the proximity of our innocent quarry. Suddenly a foot was stuck in my hurried path, a hand gave me a rough shove, and I ended sprawled on the ground, my poor damaged parcels around me like presents around a Christmas tree.

Two strong, tanned hands reached down for me, and I was gently, inexorably pulled to my feet to enjoy the quite novel sensation of looking *up* into the warmest, bluest eyes I had ever seen. I smiled up at him in dazed delight, and those beautifully shaped lips curved into an answering smile, which made the scar on his right cheek stretch and the small, fine lines around his eyes crease. And then, as if it had never been there, the smile disappeared from his face like the sun going behind a cloud, replaced by a look of stiff suspicion.

"I trust you're all right?" His voice was coolly, beautifully British, deep and rich despite his sudden, inexplicable dislike of me.

"Quite," I replied hurriedly. "Thank you so..." Before I could finish my thanks I found my arms filled with my bundles.

"Think nothing of it," he said brusquely. "But I suggest, miss, that you watch where you're going next time." And with that he disappeared into the curious crowd of shoppers, much as he had the night before.

"Well, of all the rude..." I sputtered, staring after him with indignant fascination. I had never met anyone so impolite in my short, sheltered life. It was both novel and disturbing. Added to the already upsetting effect the man had on me, it took a few moments before I realized that Maggie had reappeared at my side.

"Are you all right, Miss Luciana?" she inquired anxiously. "I hope I didn't push you too hard."

I stared at her in amazement. "Damn you, Maggie," I cursed when I got my breath back. "What an idiotic idea! I've got bruises from head to toe, a scratch on my face, our food is probably ruined..."

"But you got to meet him, didn't you?" she demanded, as if that were all that mattered.

As indeed it was. "I did. And he was abominably rude. I've quite lost interest in the man, I assure you. Mind how you carry that silk, you'll drop it!" I muttered as we threaded our way back toward the hotel. Her answer was a disbelieving laugh.

So caught up was I with indignant fascination that I failed to pay much heed to the handsome, aging gondolier who stared at us with intense interest out of moist, spaniel eyes. With a brief glance I dismissed him as one more hapless male bemused by Maggie's twitching little bottom or her companion's statuesque and overgenerous proportions. The scarred Englishman had banished all thought of my mission from my featherbrained little head.

CHAPTER FOUR

My arrival at Edentide, the ancestral home of the del Zaglias for generations untold, was hardly befitting the return of the native. Uncle Mark was up and fuming when we arrived back at the hotel and accompanied us down the wide, dark, green, and crowded expanse of the Grand Canal in a high dudgeon, scarcely replying to my commonplace pleasantries.

"You would think," he uttered in awful tones at one point, "that one of you would have more brains than a peahen. In a strange city, on a mysterious and dangerous mission, and the two of you run off like giggling schoolgirls and return loaded with dress material and tea! Absurd!"

"But, Uncle Mark," I protested sweetly, "we needed the tea. And the cleaning supplies. We could hardly set up housekeeping in a filthy dungeon without tea, could we?"

"You already know my opinion of your intended residence," he growled. "And what do you intend to do with the pink silk . . . scrub floors with it?"

"Rose silk," I corrected absently. "Maggie's going to make me a dress."

"Harrumph. So I gathered. Not that you don't sorely need one. Never saw such a shabbily dressed girl in my life. Nevertheless, your first morning in Venice is hardly the time or the place to embark on a new wardrobe."

"I disagree," Maggie piped up with her usual pertness.

"*You* would," he said morosely. "I should have known Luciana would wander off like a curious child, but I thought you would be able to exercise a little more control over her."

Maggie laughed. "Small chance of that happening, Mr. Ferland. Now or ever."

We were so busy wrangling I hadn't noticed our large and ancient gondola had pulled along a deserted, moss-coated marble quay. Looking up with a start, I had my first conscious view of Edentide in all its gloomy, ancient, marble glory.

There wasn't much color to her at this point. The last twenty years must have dealt harshly with her, for I could scarcely imagine my fastidious father inhabiting a place anywhere near this state of decrepitude. Gargoyles with chipped and broken noses adorned the corners of the top floor, the wrought-iron balustrades were rusted from the salty sea air, the shutters were closed and angry-looking.

I must have appeared somewhat daunted, for Uncle Mark let out a sour laugh of triumph. "You see what I mean? This never was a very welcoming place, even when your father made some effort to keep it up. I doubt it's even safe to walk in there anymore. I presume you've thought better of your rash plan?"

"I most certainly have not!" I climbed out of the gondola with surprising ease and scrambled onto the slippery quay. "I know perfectly well that father has sent regular sums of money to keep Edentide from sinking into the lagoon. Just enough to preserve it until the Austrians leave. I have no doubt we'll find it sturdy enough."

"And you think these villains would actually put the money to its assigned use?" he scoffed.

I met his gaze calmly. "Do you think they would dare not?" This, of course, was unanswerable, and Uncle Mark scrambled out of the gondola with far less grace than I had managed. Maggie fared worst of all, requiring the strong arms of the handsome gondolier to practically carry her onto the fondaménto.

I kept an expression of curious interest all during our long and disheartening tour of Edentide. Uncle Mark and I were both right. It *was* filthy and mildewed and rather horrid. It was also blissfully free of rats, thanks to the presence of three rather fat ginger cats with clean habits, and the floors and walls were as solid as when the first piles had been driven into the soft mud of the lagoon.

I had immediately been attracted to the small salon on the west side of the house. The walls were covered in stained golden silk, the sconces were tarnished, the furniture frayed. But once I flung open the shutters, a great deal of sunlight and fresh sea air poured in, and I was able to view the carnage around me with a bit more equanimity.

And then began the orgy of cleaning. We decided not to bother with any floor but the main one, and Maggie and I spent the next five hours scrubbing, dusting, sweeping, beating rugs, washing windows, beating feather ticks, while poor Uncle Mark was instructed to cart various articles of furniture up and down the dirty marble stairs. By the approach of five o'clock we had gotten the west salon in charming order, with a clean floor, shining sconces, scrubbed upholstery only slightly more frayed than when we had entered the house, and polished tables and desks. I sank onto a particularly inviting chaise longue, feeling incredibly tired and incredibly dirty but very pleased with myself. Maggie plopped into a chair beside me, a streak of soot across her flushed and glowing face.

The Demon Count's Daughter

Uncle Mark, ever the perfect English gentleman, lounged by the balcony, not a hair out of place, not a wrinkle in his beautifully tailored jacket.

"You seem fairly settled," he allowed handsomely. "I suppose you'll do well enough for a few nights until you tire of this roughing it. I still wish you'd reconsider and return to the hotel with me tonight."

"After all our work?" I demanded in weak outrage, too weary to protest more loudly. "Never. We have our own neat and clean bedrooms. . . ."

"With beds that I single-handedly wrestled down those damned stairs," he interrupted in a petulant voice.

"Which you nobly wrestled down the stairs," I inserted dutifully. "Even the kitchen is clean. Maggie and I will do splendidly, thank you."

"Absolutely, sir," Maggie joined in with a small show of energy. "And you can trust me to look after Miss Luciana. Lord knows I've had enough practice."

"But you weren't enough to stop her from running off with the traveling circus when she was fifteen, were you? Gone for a week before they found her, what?"

"Unfair, Uncle Mark!" I cried. "I was only gone overnight. I'd always wanted to be a tightrope walker."

"And what did your father say to that, eh? One of the blessed del Zaglias joining a circus. Bet he rung a rare peal over you that time."

"As a matter of fact he told me that if I still wanted to be a tightrope walker when I was eighteen he would see that I had lessons. I didn't, of course. And I must say, I think I've found my métier. Being a spy is a great deal of fun." My lips curved in a reminiscent smile.

"Damn it, girl, when you smile like that you look the spitting image of your mother." He shook his head. "I wish I could be easy about the two of you. At least two people that I knew personally died violent deaths in this house not twenty-five years ago."

If I was daunted I did my best not to show it. "I have no intention of following suit. You may come and check on us tomorrow morning. If you come early enough we may even feed you breakfast." I rose, and reluctantly he headed for the door, muttering dire predictions all the way out.

"And now, dear Maggie," I sighed as I wandered back in, "all I need to make me blissfully happy is a cup of strong tea, some dinner, and a bath."

"Tea, I can get you. Even dinner I can provide if you'll settle for some fried sprats and cornmeal mush. . . ."

"Polenta," I corrected gently, not at all displeased by this typical Venetian menu.

"But a bath is one thing I cannot and will not do. If you think, Miss Luciana, that I am going to heat and carry buckets and buckets of water . . ."

"No, no, no," I soothed her. "Just wishful thinking. I feel so dirty; there's nothing I'd like more than . . ." I broke off as a delightfully wicked idea came to my ever-active imagination.

"I don't like that look in your eye, Miss Luciana. It bodes ill for someone."

"Pish and tush," I replied. "I am going to get clean, and in the easiest way possible. I'm going swimming."

"Where?" she demanded, and then a look of dawning horror appeared on her face. "Oh, no, miss. You can't mean it! Not in this dirty canal water."

"I certainly do. Father used to swim here all the time. I saw some boys swimming when we arrived. The canal on the side of the house is deserted . . . no houses or windows face on it but ours. And it will be a very short swim."

"I've never known you to take a short swim. I think you must be part eel yourself. And you're far more likely to come out dirtier than when you went in."

"Ah, but Maggie, you don't understand the secret of the Venetian garbage system. The ebb tide carries all the trash and sewage out into the open sea every day, and the return is fresh, clean sea water. Can't you smell . . . the tide has just come in." I took an appreciative sniff of the clean, watery smell, and Maggie took a disdainful sniff of disapproval.

"You're mad, Miss Luciana. But there's no telling you. Go on ahead—I can't stop you. But you'll have to sleep in your canal slime . . . I've told you already I won't get you a bath."

It took all my powers of persuasion to convince Maggie to accompany me down the long, dark, dank passageway that led under the house to the side entrance. Various rustlings in the dark left me with the gloomy conviction that the cats had not been quite as efficient as I had hoped, and the green moss growing along the sturdy and uncracked marble foundations added to the eerie atmosphere of the place. If I hadn't made such an issue of swimming in the first place, I would have suggested we turn back.

"Gawd, this is an awful place, ain't it?" Maggie whispered as we neared the end of the pathway. "I wouldn't like to be locked down here on a stormy night."

"Don't!" I shuddered. "We mustn't be superstitious. It's just another part of the house—a little bit damper, but nothing else."

"Isn't this where your father killed the—?"

"Please, Maggie!" I shrieked, and my voice echoed down the cavernous crypt. "I'd rather not think about it." Thankfully, I swung open the old and rusty door after a nervous moment fiddling with the bolts. "That was all a long time ago. It really shouldn't bother us in the least."

"Well, it bothers me. And what bothers me more, Miss Luciana, is what you're intending to wear for this twilight swim you're planning." She cast a suspicious glance over my rumpled skirt and blouse. "I hope you have more sense than to consider going in the altogether. That's bad enough in Somerset, but here with those Eyetalian brigands . . ." She shivered in delicious anticipation, obviously longing to run into an Eyetalian brigand in the altogether.

"But Maggie, I'd drown if I wore all this," I pointed out with great practicality.

"You've got a chemise on, haven't you? And pantalets? Indecent, of course, but better than nothing." I was quickly peeling off the grime-stained outer layers, and I nodded in compliance. The chemise was made of fine lawn and Venetian lace and came to just above my knees; the pantalets were short and frilly and absurdly dainty.

When wet, I knew they would be just as bad as the infamous "altogether," but I didn't bother informing Maggie of that fact. I sat down on the moss-coated quayside and dangled my bare feet into the splendidly cool salt water.

"I don't really fancy waiting alone in this great dark hole while you paddle around," Maggie warned. "In and out—that's all the swimming you'll do today, my girl."

"Yes, Maggie," I replied meekly, taking the pins out of my heavy hair and letting it hang like a thick, black curtain down my back. We were far enough away from the lights and noises of the Grand Canal so that I felt completely private. Especially now, at what appeared to be the dinner hour for so many of my fellow Venetians. Bracing myself against the dock, I slid slowly and quietly into the cool, green depths, letting out a long sigh of pure delight before taking off in strong, rapid strokes toward the end of the house.

"That's enough, Miss Luciana," Maggie called out uneasily. "Come back now."

"I can't!" I protested. "I've barely cooled off. Give me a few minutes more, Maggie."

"I don't like it here. Come now, or I'll leave you. I swear I will."

"Go ahead!" I called gaily, forgetting the eerie

passageway and its ancient ghosts. "I'll be in directly."

"Miss Luciana, come now!" There was thunder in Maggie's voice, a thunder I chose to ignore.

"Go ahead and start supper, Maggie," I replied, floating on my back and wiggling my toes. "Or else you can come in and fetch me," I added wickedly, knowing how Maggie detested water in any form other than a tepid bath.

"Damn you, then!" she cried, and vanished from the dockside. I did a shallow dive and began a leisurely examination of the underside of Venice. When I surfaced for air the side of the old house looked different. It took me a full minute to realize that the water door was firmly closed, with no outside handle. It took only a small push from the water to ascertain that it was indeed locked.

CHAPTER FIVE

For a long moment panic set in, and I sank beneath the salty waters of the lagoon like an idiot. I surfaced quickly, coughing and sputtering and choking, my eyes stinging from the bite of the salt. Placing two hands on the moss-covered marble quay, I tried to pull my tired and frightened body upward. But the seaweed growing in slimy profusion gave me no purchase, and I slipped back beneath the now treacherous waters, my hands scrabbling desperately at the dock. Again I surfaced and tried to crawl out, again I felt my hands slip, my nails tearing helplessly. I tried to call for help, but the exhaustion of the past week and day had caught up with me with evil speed, and all that came forth before I slipped beneath the canal was a hoarse croak.

While my body was weakening my mind was working feverishly. I wasted valuable time cursing myself for being a careless idiot, for trying to swim in an unfamiliar place when I had already pushed myself too far and too fast. And as I made my way wearily to the blessed surface, I weakly realized it might be the last time.

Blinded by the sea water and desperation, I reached out one last time for the marble fondaménto, gulping in the sweet night air. Once more I felt myself begin to slip, and I resigned myself to an early, albeit fitting, watery grave when suddenly I felt my weak wrists gripped tightly by two iron hands.

It was then I began to struggle in earnest until a deep, sure British voice that I recognized instantly cut through my panic. "Calm down," he ordered sternly. "I've got a hold of you. You'll be out in a moment. Just take deep, slow breaths."

Numbly I complied, and in a few seconds I felt myself being pulled out of the water with a sudden jerk of quite impressive strength and dumped on the slime-covered quay.

I lay there in a wet and sorry heap, my breath coming in long shudders, my body trembling from the aftermath of fear and the suddenly chill night air. My rescuer knelt beside me, and as I turned to thank him I came face to face with the angriest blue eyes I had ever seen.

"Do you realize," he began in an icy voice, stripping off his jacket to reveal a set of powerfully built shoulders, "what an idiotic, dangerous thing that was for you to do? A child would have more sense than to go swimming unattended in a strange place." While his voice was rough with anger, his hands were gentle as they lifted me and drew the warm linen jacket around my shivering body. "You should have some sort of keeper, someone to make sure you get into no more trouble. Venice is a dangerous place for fools and innocents."

"Which am I?" I questioned weakly, not really minding his harangue as long as he kept those gentle, reassuring hands on me. Both my parents had hot tempers, and I had come to associate being yelled at with people who loved me. I felt positively cherished as the nameless, scarred Englishman lit it into me.

"Both," he snapped, smoothing my wet, tangled hair away from my face. "You should turn around and go straight back to England," he said in a milder tone. "This is no place for you."

"How do you know I've come from England?" I questioned with spylike surprise, remembering my duties belatedly.

He hesitated for only a moment. "You know as well as I do that I saw you arrive last night. And your voice is as unmistakably British as your face is Venetian."

I smiled at that, obscurely pleased. "Well, I can't go back to England right now, even if I wanted to. I have business here."

"You are far too young to have business that couldn't be better conducted by the men in your family," he said in an oppressive voice.

"I am just as capable as the men in my family," I snapped, struggling out of my very comfortable position, which was half in his arms.

A look of amusement passed over his aloof face. "God help your family, then." He helped me to my less-than-steady feet, catching his jacket deftly as it slid off my shoulders. "Are you quite all right?" A note of concern had slipped beneath his cold reserve, and it warmed me despite the chill damp of my skin.

"I'm fine," I replied, holding out my hand politely. "And once more I must thank you, Mr. . . . ?" I let it trail meaningfully.

The mocking smile was very much in evidence now as he took my hand to his lips and kissed it with the lightest of touches. "I would suggest, Miss del Zaglia, that you keep my jacket for now. Your costume, though extremely attractive, is a bit too revealing for polite society, even in Venice."

I looked down at the sheer, clinging lawn that covered my ripe curves, and a warm blush mounted to my cheeks and spread all over the large expanse of visible skin. Snatching back his jacket, I pulled it around me in sudden and unusual modesty, barely managing to stammer out my thanks.

It suddenly seemed very still and quiet, alone with him on the slime-covered fondaménto outside the austere and gloomy environs of the palazzo Edentide on a cool August night. The sounds of the Grand Canal seemed small and far away, and I had the odd, by no means unpleasant, feeling that we were alone to the world, my nameless scarred Englishman and I. And I knew with an ancient and sure instinct that he had the same eerie feeling. A gentle hand came under my chin, drawing me up to face those deep, troubled eyes as his other hand once more smoothed my wet locks from my face. The smell of the sea was strong on my skin and his hand, and the soft night breeze played through his dark gold hair, ruffling it just slightly.

"Take care, Luciana," he said in a soft voice, and my stomach seemed to contract within me. "The world is full of cruel, evil people, people who want to hurt innocent young girls like you. Take care," he repeated gently, his hand an unconscious caress on my cheek.

"I can look after myself," I replied in a hushed, but firm, tone.

He looked down at my damp, scanty clothing, barely covered by the warm folds of his jacket.

"Really?" he said skeptically. "I do hope so, Luciana. I do hope so."

A sudden scraping at the door brought us both out of our reverie, and in a moment he was gone, swiftly and silently, so that were it not for the warm, soft folds of his coat around me, I would have thought I had dreamed his presence.

"Are you all right, Miss Luciana?" Maggie demanded, peering through the gathering dusk. "I thought I heard someone walking around upstairs, calling me. It must have been my imagination, for no one was there. When I came back down the door here was shut and locked." She couldn't quite keep the worry out of her voice.

I moved into sight, careful to keep a matter-of-fact note in my somewhat shaky voice. "I'm fine, Maggie. I had a little trouble climbing back out onto the fondaménto, but a gentleman helped me."

"What gentleman?" she demanded suspiciously, squinting down the canal.

A seraphic smile creased my lips as I preceded her into the dark, damp cellars of the palazzo. The cellars that had seen death already in this century. "You owe me another dress," I said sweetly.

With a great deal more bravado than wisdom Maggie and I both came to the comforting conclusion that the nonexistent wind had shut the heavy, rusted sea door, with the force of it closing the sticky latch once more. That selfsame wind was also responsible for the voices and footsteps that had called Maggie away from my side—an illusion, nothing more. In the meantime, however, we locked and bolted the sturdy door down into the cellars, and every few minutes one of us would cast a nervous glance in the general direction of the wide marble stairs, expecting heaven knows what sort of ghost to make its sepulchral way down the recently dusted steps.

Between the two of us we managed a creditable job of the sprats and polenta. By the time we had finished eating a disgustingly huge amount, drunk several quarts of strong tea, and washed the dishes, bed seemed like a most pleasant place to be. It took all of Maggie's powers of persuasion to talk me into staying up another hour and helping her cut out the first of my dresses, and by nine o'clock I flatly refused to do anything more on it.

"I'm exhausted," I complained bitterly, struggling to my feet and staring down at the scraps of rose-colored silk that would somehow, inexplicably, become an exceedingly flattering dress.

"I never thought to hear you say that, Miss Luciana," Maggie replied pertly from her kneeling position, her mouth full of pins. "Go on to bed, then; I'll be along shortly." She let out a short, sharp laugh. "And don't think I don't know why you're so eager to go to bed for once."

"Whatever do you mean?"

"You want to dream of your handsome pirate. Well, it can do no harm," she observed magnanimously. "And once we have you looking more like a lady . . . well, who knows what will happen? I think, Miss Luciana, that you should just forget why you came here and concentrate on that gentleman. Spying's no ladylike occupation. You should be married and have one or two little ones running around by your age."

The thought of marriage with the aloof Englishman was curiously enticing, and reluctantly I put a tight rein on my imagination. "I can't forget why I'm here, Maggie. No matter how much I'm tempted, no matter how much I wish I could, I can't." Unconsciously I stiffened my backbone. "Good night, Maggie." The only reply was a derisive snort.

My small, neat bedroom had obviously been a dining salon at one point. Most of the furniture had been too rickety to be of much use, and Uncle Mark had obligingly dragged it off to the section of the cellars I had designated for storage. Instead of wobbling, frayed furniture, the room now boasted a small, ornately carved wooden bed with plain white cotton hangings to protect me from the noxious sea airs, a plain table and chair, an armoire, which had required Maggie's and my help in wresting it from one of the second-floor bedrooms, and a small, very old, and exquisitely beautiful Oriental rug. Maggie had closed the shutters to the small balcony, effectively cutting off any fresh air on this close, still night. The balcony overlooked the side canal that had almost caused my death that evening; but looking down at it from the safe height of my room, it seemed calm and gentle and once more welcoming on such a sticky night. Firmly I put that thought from my mind, blew out my lamp, and undressed slowly and thoughtfully in the dark. I was asleep in a few short minutes.

I felt the bed sag beneath his weight as he sat down by my sleeping body. Those hands that had rescued me from a watery grave were warm and gentle on my face, waking me just enough so that I turned and offered my mouth to his insistent touch. I could feel the weight of his lips on mine, and I let out a little sigh of pure pleasure as I squirmed like a kitten.

His mouth left mine and traveled in short, delicate kisses, over my cheeks, my eyes, my brow, my soft, silky hair, as his hands gently pulled away the thin cotton sheet that lay over my nude body. He pulled it only as far as my hips, and then his mouth moved down my neck, leaving a trail of fire in its wake as he drew me up into his arms.

I lay there for a moment, enjoying the feel of his arms around me, his mouth on my neck. And then the feel of those strong, beautiful hands on my naked skin awoke a response in me I barely knew existed. His wrists lay against my breasts, and I reached my arms around his neck and drew his closer, closer, until we were kissing once more, his mouth hot and demanding, his warm, clever hands on my breasts causing me an almost unbearable mixture of pain and pleasure.

I let my untutored mouth trace the thin, angry line of his scar, and then his head moved down, down, until his lips found my full breasts, bared beneath his touch, and his hungry mouth fastened on my taut and straining nipples, kneading, sucking, and biting them, until I moaned aloud with delight. I laced my fingers through his thick, long hair and held him closer, ever closer to me, writhing on the bed as he pulled the sheet away from the rest of me, his lips . . .

The yowl of a Venetian alley cat brought me suddenly, swiftly, horribly awake, and I lay alone in my narrow bed, the sheet at my feet, covered with a thin glow of sweat, trembling with the chill of the night air. A dream. It had all been a licentious, voluptuous, embarrassing, delectable dream. I wanted to cry out in rage and frustration.

A shudder passed over my body, swiftly followed by another and then another. Stumbling from my bed I crossed the mosaic floor on bare feet and found the armoire in the fitful moonlight. I took the Englishman's coat from its hook and wrapped it around my naked, shivering body. Climbing back into my soft bed, I heaved a sigh that was an odd mixture of contentment, relief, and disappointment. And in another moment I was sound asleep, this time for the remainder of the warm and sultry Venetian night, whose warmth could turn suddenly, bitingly chill.

CHAPTER SIX

I slept later than usual the next morning. By the time I struggled out of bed, forced a comb through my salt-tangled hair and arranged it in a simple manner, threw on a wrapper, and washed my face, it was close to ten o'clock. I found Maggie sitting in the salon, sewing industriously on the rose-colored silk, a cup of tea at her left elbow, her neat little feet perched on a petit point stool only slightly frayed from age and damp.

"You look quite demure this morning," I observed, pouring myself a blessedly strong cup of tea. "How long have you been up?" I wandered over to stare out at the noise and bustle of the Grand Canal.

"Any number of hours now, Miss Luciana. I've been to the square to buy milk from those cunning little milkmaids, I've had breakfast, and made a great deal of progress on this dress." She held it up for my inspection, and indeed, it had begun to take shape in an amazingly short amount of time. "And you've received an invitation."

I turned back quickly, almost spilling my tea. "Already?" I exclaimed, remembering my seemingly futile trip to the Merceria yesterday and Tonetti's secretive note. "From Tonetti?"

"I sincerely doubt it," she replied wryly. "It's from the embassy. Lady Bute, the consul's wife, to be exact. For tea this afternoon; I was so bold as to tell the messenger you'd be pleased to attend. I think we can thank your Uncle Mark for that particular attention. Lady Bute was one of his old flirts."

"How do you know that?"

She waved an airy hand. "Servants have ways of picking up on things," she replied, looking in no way like a servant in her elegant green muslin dress that was deliberately cut just a trifle too low for daytime wear. "You know what that invitation means, don't you?"

"I haven't the faintest idea, other than a possibly boring afternoon with a bunch of stuffy people," I said rudely. Formal teas had long been a bane of my existence, providing far more punishment than pleasure, and I wasn't looking forward to this afternoon's treat.

"It's Lady Bute's official monthly tea," Maggie explained with great patience. "All those people who are anybody will be invited. Including your mysterious friend who arrives so opportunely."

She made a neat little knot and cast a suspicious glance at my happy face. "You needn't be quite so jolly, Miss Luciana. He might not be there."

"No, you're right, Maggie." I waltzed around the room in the strong Venetian sunlight. "He'll be there, I know he will. I . . . I don't suppose there's any chance the dress . . . ?"

"Will be finished in time?" she continued for me. "Why do you think I'm sitting here on such a glorious day? I may have to sew you into it, but you'll have it to wear this afternoon. Your Uncle Mark will be calling for you at three."

I swooped down and gave her an exuberant hug, careful to watch my surprising strength or I could have cracked a few ribs. "Bless you, Maggie! What more could I ask?"

"That we get out of this devilish situation your impulsiveness hurled us into with our skins intact," she suggested morosely.

That afternoon I dressed with far greater care than I usually expended and consequently Uncle Mark was left cooling his heels in the salon for a good twenty minutes while Maggie sewed me into the rose-silk dress. She had done an admirable job of it—the soft folds hugged my uncorseted body and draped gracefully around my narrow hoops. The deep fold of Venetian lace around the shoulders set off the warm tones of my skin to perfection, and as I moved it rustled in a soft, feminine manner. We had worked a full hour on my thick, straight black hair. The damp sea air had given it more weight than usual, and as Maggie twined and plaited and pinned, small tendrils escaped the severe style and framed my face in a flattering fashion. I applied rose hips to my cheeks, charcoal to my already dark lashes, gardenia scent to my wrists, breasts, and the nape of my neck. When I was finished Maggie drew back and looked at me in astonishment.

"My Gawd, Miss Luciana," she breathed in amazement.

"What's wrong? Don't I look pretty?" I demanded, worried that I had been too partial to my reflection in the gold leaf mirror.

Maggie shook her curly head. "No, dearie, you aren't pretty. Not a bit." She laughed as my mouth drooped. "You are absolutely beautiful. I never knew you could be such a looker."

"You swine!" I shook her. "You frightened me for a moment." I pranced in front of my reflection, turning my full, graceful skirts this way and that. "Will he think so too?"

Maggie had no doubts as to the identity of "he." "He'd be half-mad not to. You look just like that picture your pa has in his study. Of the lady."

"The Giorgione Madonna?" I supplied, amazed. "I really do? She's beautiful!"

"And so are you," Maggie said stoutly. "If you'd just keep those spirits under control. You have the same serene sort of looks. When you aren't being wicked, that is."

"I'll work on it, Maggie," I promised solemnly, turning to give myself one last smug grin in the tarnished surface of the mirror.

Uncle Mark's reaction was fully as flattering as Maggie's, though not quite so amazed. "I always knew you were a beauty," he said loyally, helping me into the gondola with surprisingly careful hands. "How could you help but be, with parents like yours?"

This was unanswerable, and the trip to the British Consulate was quick and silent. Uncle Mark seemed vague and abstracted; even more so than usual. Only once did he break the stillness.

"You still haven't heard from Tonetti, have you?"

I started guiltily, then met his worried blue eyes with a limpid expression. I had already determined not to confide in anyone if I could help it, smugly certain I could handle it far better without his meddling. Besides, I told myself virtuously, he would only worry needlessly. "I haven't heard anything yet," I replied with sweet innocence. "I expect to any day now."

"I don't understand it," he said worriedly, more to himself than to me. "I would have thought someone would have made contact by now. We've been here almost forty-eight hours—usually these people don't waste any time." He sighed, looking at the magic city as we glided by with blind eyes. "I can't rest easy until I've gotten you safely back in Somerset. This was a crazy idea to begin with. Bones must be senile!"

I listened to him in silence. "What's done is done," I said with great originality. "We should hear something soon. No doubt we'll be back in England before you know it."

"I only hope it's before your father knows it. I shudder to think of his reaction when he finds I've accompanied you here."

I patted his hand reassuringly. "His reaction would be far worse if he found that you had let me go alone."

"Yes, that's true," he muttered, brightening somewhat. My father had the ability to terrify most of his acquaintances when he chose to, and Mark Ferland was particularly vulnerable.

I stirred uneasily, and the gondola rocked slightly as it sliced through the dark green salt water. "Well, it should all be cleared up in a while," I said optimistically, wondering whether I ought to take Uncle Mark into my confidence. Despite his vague demeanor, he had some experience in the field. I sat there in a quandary, unable to make up my mind.

"I must say Venice agrees with you," my godfather continued thoughtfully after a moment. "Perhaps Bones knew what he was doing after all when he sent you. I only wish he'd had the foresight to send someone along to protect you."

But didn't he send you, I thought suddenly? And if not, who and where was the watchdog Bones had promised me? I opened my mouth to question him when the gondola pulled up along the quay outside the British Consulate, and in the bustle of disembarking and greeting our various fellow guests, all of whom seemed to know Uncle Mark and my parents intimately, the subject was lost, not to return until late that night when I was alone and half-asleep.

We were halfway across the formal receiving room on the third floor of the old palazzo that had become the consulate, making our leisurely way to greet our hostess, Lady Bute, when I whispered uneasily to my godfather, "Everyone is staring at me. I must look a freak in this pink dress." Years of doubt and horrid self-consciousness about my unusual height came flooding back to me, and I felt like sinking through the polished marble floor.

Uncle Mark stopped short, turning amazed eyes on me. "My dear girl, they're not staring at you because you're tall—they're staring at you because you're beautiful. Remember, Luciana," he admonished sternly, "you're a del Zaglia."

Unconsciously I threw back my shoulders and smiled at the assembled multitude. The number of smiles I received in return amazed me.

"My God," I whispered, amazed, "I believe you're right, Uncle Mark."

Lady Bute was a very carefully preserved blonde somewhere on the shady side of fifty. She greeted her old beau, Uncle Mark, with a noisy and enthusiastic kiss on the lips and looked as if she were about to bestow the same salute on me upon our introduction. I quickly proffered my cheek, clanging into her chin with jarring force, and then drew back, aghast at my unusual clumsiness.

Lady Bute, far from being irritated, let out a high little trill of laughter, squeezed my hand with surprising strength, and waved my godfather away with one plump, bejeweled wrist. "You are Luc and Carlotta's daughter! How I've longed to meet you, my dear. No one ever told me you were such a beauty . . . every eye is upon you today. I feel quite put out."

No one had ever told me I was a beauty, either, I thought, and then realized that was untrue. My parents had always made me feel exquisitely lovely. It was only when I was away from their protective, sheltering love that I felt overgrown and lost the natural grace that was mine.

"Sit beside me, my child, and we shall enjoy a great gossip. There's nothing I don't know about who's in Venice, and I'm dying to hear the latest from your dear family. How many brothers do you have now? Was it three?"

"Six," I replied, smiling. "The youngest is Marco, who's barely a year and a half."

"Your mother never ceases to amaze me," she said sincerely. "The lucky creature."

We passed the next half hour in an extremely agreeable fashion. It seemed there were very few people present at the formal tea who hadn't a scandal hidden deep in their past, a scandal Lady Bute had managed to unearth long ago. So fascinated was I in all this that I failed to notice Uncle Mark's defection with a pretty, blue-haired widow, or the arrival of my mysterious gentleman, until a pause in Lady Bute's voluble conversation allowed me to cast a casual eye over the proceedings.

From my vantage point in the little alcove at the head of the room I could see him clearly, towering over the various international guests with easy grace. As far as I could tell he had yet to see me. Or if he had, he hadn't cared, I thought morosely.

"Who are you looking at with such a curious expression, my dear?" Lady Bute demanded, her long nose itching for more gossip. "Do I detect an expression of romantic longing on your lovely young face? You shouldn't be so transparent, my girl. Gentlemen should be kept guessing."

Blushing, I tried to deny any romantic interest. As my protests came out in stammered half-phrases, an old campaigner like Lady Bute was not fooled for a minute.

"I beg you, darling, tell me who he is! I can be discreet, I promise you." Unlikely chance, I thought cynically, closing my mouth tight against my usual longing to confide in anyone or anything. "I do so love romance," she twittered on. "Is it an attachment of long standing?"

I had to laugh. "It isn't an attachment at all, my lady. I was merely curious about one of your guests." Should I keep my mouth shut or should I not? I wondered feverishly beneath my calm expression. I doubted I would find such a gold mine of information again. And what harm would it do if she knew of my interest? I would be gone from Venice in a few short days, never to return until the Austrians had finally departed.

Lady Bute's sharp little eyes, like hard, shiny marbles, followed the direction of my limpid gaze, and widened in consternation. "Evan Fitzpatrick!" she exclaimed in an undertone, and I turned to her eagerly.

"Is that his name? I've seen him any number of times since I've arrived, but we've yet to be introduced. Would you . . . ?"

"Introduce you? Never," she said flatly, a deceptively merry expression in those eyes.

"But why not?"

"My duties as the wife of the consul, my dear, do not include introducing young ladies of proper upbringing to men who are scarcely gentlemen."

"Scarcely gentlemen?" I echoed, puzzled. "He seems perfectly genteel enough. I don't understand."

"You've talked with him?" she edged closer. "My goodness, what an intrigue! I didn't know Evan had ever bothered to exchange more than two words with a young lady of virtuous ways. This is absolutely fascinating. Tell me, where did you meet him?"

"At the Merceria," I replied. "And the train station. And outside Edentide." For the first time the coincidence seemed unpleasantly striking. "He's very rude," I added.

"Yes, that's Evan," the older woman said fondly. "Hated you on sight, didn't he?"

I remembered his gentle hands smoothing away my sea-damp hair, the look of concern in his angry, silver-blue eyes. I smiled reflectively. "Well, no, not really," I allowed.

"Then you've worked some sort of spell on him," she said flatly.

"Why? Why won't you introduce me to him, why is he not quite a gentleman, why should he hate me on sight?" I demanded, unable to tear my eyes away from the back of his neck, the lovely way the overlong dark blond hair curled around his collar, the deceptive strength in those shoulders.

Lady Bute hesitated for only a moment. "Very well, my dear. I will tell you what I know of Evan Fitzpatrick, and then you will see just how totally ineligible he is. We shall take a short stroll on the north terrace, where we are unlikely to be interrupted. Come with me." She rose to her small height with classic dignity, and I followed suit, towering over her and feeling like a giantess. "My, you are a Juno, aren't you?" she said sweetly, drawing her arm through mine and leading me away from the multitude out onto the flowered terrace.

"To begin with," she said in a lowered voice once we were alone, "he is divorced." The tones she spoke in suggested an axe murderer at the very least, and I sighed with relief.

"Is that all?"

"Isn't that enough? But no, that is not all. England must have changed if the young people accept divorce so easily. In my day divorced people were not received."

"But you receive Evan Fitzpatrick?" I pointed out.

A sly smile creased her aging face. "Indeed, I do. But you'll find, my dear, that there are very few men as handsome as Evan Fitzpatrick that I don't receive. But I also do not introduce them to the innocent daughters of the nobility, be they Venetian or English."

"And what else is so horrid about him?" I demanded, feeling absurdly protective. "Did he abandon his poor, frail, helpless wife?"

"As a matter of fact Amelia was the most ghastly bitch. She had the morals of a Roman, and didn't bother to hide it. Daughter of a duke, but the most ill-bred creature I have ever met. She gave Evan that attractive scar, you know. I believe she did it with a letter opener."

"My God," I whispered in horror. "Is that when he divorced her?"

"Heavens, no! It wasn't until two or three years after that. They have a son. Sweet young boy, I believe; goes to school in England somewhere. It wasn't talked about openly, and the divorce trial was closed, but I have friends in high places. It turned out that the dear Amelia had a particularly nasty habit of having her five-year-old son watch while she disported with her current lover. Or lovers, as the case may have been. If the poor child was uncooperative she would fly into one of her maniacal rages. I gather she broke his arm in three places. *That* was when Evan divorced her."

I felt like throwing up. "I would have murdered her," I said quietly.

"Well, as a matter of fact, there was some question of that. A few years after the divorce she was found strangled in a Paris bordello which catered to odd tastes. No one was ever caught, but it was rumored that Evan might have finally gotten his revenge. He was wandering around Europe at the time. Still is, I suppose, though he's been in Venice for almost a year now."

"And for divorcing that . . . that monster of depravity he's ostracized from society?" I demanded, outraged.

Lady Bute shrugged, leaning against the marble balustrade and plucking a bright orange nasturtium from the flower box. "Such is the way of the world, my dear. There are certain rules, and if we relax them, civilization will topple."

"Civilization will not topple if people are sympathetic to a man who's obviously been through hell," I said crossly.

"Sympathetic?" she echoed, amused. "He wouldn't thank you for that, my dear. And I have a double reason for not introducing you. He detests women. Ever since Amelia he's decided we're all either sluts, teases, deviants, or useless, idle gossips." I could recognize who fell into that last category. "You wouldn't get a decent word out of him."

"I've already had several."

My companion sighed gustily. "Perhaps you're the one to convince him he's wrong about our fair sex. I must confess, if I were unmarried and ten years younger, I'd be tempted to give it a try myself. I do so love a rake."

"A rake! I thought you said he hated women?"

She smiled, a sly, secret smile. "But those, my dear, are the best kind."

CHAPTER SEVEN

There was no changing Lady Bute's determination not to introduce me to my scarred Englishman. I couldn't help but wonder whether jealousy might be behind it.

"Well, then, I will simply have to introduce myself," I declared sweetly, heading back toward the gathering.

"You wouldn't dare!" Lady Bute scurried to catch up with me, dropping the torn petals on the marble terrace, her expression both aghast and amused. "My dear, remember, you're a del Zaglia!"

"That's exactly what I am remembering," I replied stoutly. "My parents would never approve of ignoring a man for such idiotic reasons."

A note of panic crept into my companion's voice as she placed a restraining, jeweled hand upon my arm. "I'm not saying you should ignore him. If you meet him you should nod pleasantly and walk on. But to actually seek out his company . . ." She shuddered delicately, and I laughed.

"Never fear, Lady Bute," I reassured her, detaching her clinging hands with gentle strength, "the Lord protects fools and innocents. And I have it on the best authority that I'm both."

As I started off toward my quarry I thought I heard her mutter, "No doubt." But I was set upon my course by this time and ignored the carping remark.

Evan Fitzpatrick was standing in a corner, deep in conversation with a voluptuous blonde lady in an indecently low-cut dress for that hour of the day. As far as I could tell he was completely unaware of my presence, but instinctively I knew that was untrue. He was as fully aware of me as I was of him, and the thought both frightened and warmed me.

As I neared his corner of the room some of my bravado had begun to fade. I could scarcely barge into the middle of his seemingly fascinating conversation, hold out one slender hand, and announce my name. Besides, in some obscure manner he already seemed to know who I was.

I cast a desperate glance around the room, hoping to find Uncle Mark. He could perform the introductions I so desperately wanted. But his graying head was nowhere in sight, nor was there anyone else with whom I was more than casually acquainted.

From out of nowhere a cup of tea was thrust at me, and unthinkingly I accepted it, not bothering to see who offered it. I took a large gulp out of the strong, peaty stuff, my eyes still upon my quarry.

Another swallow and absently I glanced down at the saucer in my hand, and the small twist of paper that was rapidly soaking up the slopped-over tea.

In the blink of an eye I had the damp missive safely tucked in my ever-present reticule, my heart beating faster than usual as I glanced around me with feigned interest. For a moment all thought of Evan Fitzpatrick fled my mind as I searched the crowds for a suspicious face. Everyone seemed intent on their own concerns, and I moved closer to Evan and his obviously Austrian harlot.

I edged near enough so that I could hear his voice, that cool, clipped, British voice, which for some reason had the power to move me more than any voice I had ever heard. His scarred side was toward me, and once more I wondered at his disfigurement's ability to render him even more attractive. At that moment his eyes met mine, then passed over me with complete and bone-chilling indifference.

I stood there in helpless hurt, stunned at his cool disdain. For a moment I imagined how amused Lady Bute would be. Having informed me that it was my duty to give Evan the cut direct, she would be delighted to know that *he* had taken that prerogative.

Momentarily downcast, I searched around for a quick exit before I made a complete fool of myself. A very handsome, somewhat overscented Venetian manservant of uncertain age hovered nearby. As my eyes met his he immediately began bearing down on me, a large silver tray full of teacups and cookies balanced precariously. The crowds thinned out in front of him, and he continued forward, obviously with the blissful assumption that all would move out of his elegantly graceful way. My evil half took over, my delicate foot slipped out, and the servant, the tray, and all its contents crashed into Evan Fitzpatrick and his companion, covering the sensuous blonde with crumbs and tea, staining her low-cut lavender dress and dowsing her elaborate curls. Evan had moved in time, receiving the dregs of a cup or two, and my own rose silk escaped with only a drop or two on the hem.

The blonde shrieked in German words no lady should ever use, and I was doubly glad I had managed to inundate both a hated Austrian and an inamorata of my Englishman. I turned suddenly, and my self-satisfied smirk met his cool, deep blue eyes. Immediately I changed my expression to one of deep concern, but it was too late. A look of reluctant amusement crept into his eyes, and a slight smile curved his molded lips. Grinning back unashamedly, I turned and swept away from the melee, pleased to have survived, and even won, that last encounter.

Uncle Mark was waiting for me on the side terrace. "What's all that screeching in there?" he demanded. "Never heard such a racket in all my life. These parties are getting damnably underbred."

I thought of Evan, and barely controlled my impulse to rise to his defense. Mark had disappeared so early, he probably hadn't even noticed his presence.

"Some Austrian lady," I replied calmly. "And I use the term 'lady' very loosely, indeed. A servant spilled a tray of tea and cookies all over her." I smiled.

Uncle Mark met that smile. "Assisted by a certain young English lady, no doubt?"

I nodded, descending the polished marble steps. "Do you know, uncle, I feel more and more Venetian the longer I stay here? And yet I also feel more and more British. It's very confusing."

"I dare say," he replied absently. "That's what comes of intermarriage. Now if your mother had seen fit to marry me . . ." He handed me into the gondola.

"Then you would have had a nice, placid, blonde English daughter," I completed the sentence. "With no such problems to contend with."

"I would hope," he said sincerely, "that our daughter would have been just like you."

I was touched, but couldn't help laughing. "I doubt you would, dear uncle. I am very much my father's daughter. If your wife had given birth to me there would be little doubt as to what she'd been doing nine months before."

"Luciana!" Uncle Mark protested, deeply shocked. His outrage was enough to last the trip back to the slime-covered portal of Edentide, but it also fortunately rescued him from his ever-increasing sentimental moods. It was all I could do to be polite and leisurely with the latest missive burning a hole in my reticule and my patience. By some stroke of fortune he decided to leave me at the door, and it took only a small amount of subterfuge to escape Maggie's watchful eye long enough to untwist the sodden piece of paper and decipher the blurred message.

"My beloved! I long for a brief word, a glance, a touch! A midnight rendezvous would greatly benefit many people. Be so good as to wear a mask and domino. A gondolier will be waiting by the

Rio di S. Felice at eleven thirty. Be there, or I will throw myself into the canals. Your most devoted servant, Enrico Tonetti."

The note was poorly spelled as before, and I was more conscious than anything of a feeling of desperate uncertainty. I longed more than anything to crumple the thinly veiled instructions and grind them beneath my heelless morocco slippers.

Quickly I pulled myself together, casting a speaking glance at my misty-eyed reflection in the gilt mirror. "For shame, Luciana!" I scolded in a soft voice. "What would Bones think of you, ready to abandon the future of Venice for the sake of a pair of silver-blue eyes? What would your ancestors think, one of which was a cousin to a doge? What would Luc think? What would your mother think?"

Ah, but Carlotta Theresa Sabina Morrow del Zaglia would understand very well, I realized, thinking of my mother with belated fondness. But I knew with a sinking certainty that if I abandoned my quest, even if they all forgave me, I would never forgive myself.

Crumpling the note slowly, I was brutally aware of how alone and unprotected I was. I wished more than anything that Evan Fitzpatrick would appear as suddenly and mysteriously as he had already in the past two days, watching over me as I entered into the lion's den.

I dressed once more in one of my bottle-green dresses, hanging the rose silk in the cupboard with meticulous care. Maggie's questions seemed to have no end, and I answered them the best I could as I ate a nervous, scanty meal in the west salon and prepared for my first crack at espionage.

"Well, then, Miss Luciana," Maggie demanded as she finished the last of the fried eels that somehow failed to excite my appetite, "what do you think of him now? Don't you think you might do better with one of those nice young men from home that have been buzzing around you this past year or more? Johnny Phillips or the Viscount Herington?" She knew the answer before I even spoke it. A lifetime together banishes a lot of surprises.

"Maggie," I said in a quiet, determined voice. "I think you should be the first to know. Once I'm finished here in Venice I intend to marry Evan Fitzpatrick or damned well die trying."

An unreadable expression passed over Maggie's pert face. "And what do you think your parents will say to that?" she questioned prosaically.

"I don't care. I think they'll trust my judgment, but if not . . ." I shrugged, signaling my unconcern. "The main person I have to convince is the bridegroom."

"Yes, well, that might take some doing. You won't get very far without his consent, and, if you don't mind my saying so, you haven't much experience with the ways of the opposite sex. You have to handle them very carefully to get them to do what you want—you have to convince them it was their idea in the first place."

I shook my head, smiling. "No, Maggie. I have no intention of tricking him. I will simply show him that he can't live without me."

"And how do you intend to do that? By knocking tea trays over his lady friends?"

I thought back to his amused smile, and my lips curved softly. "Perhaps. I'll simply have to take each day as it comes. Would you care to place a little wager on the outcome?" I questioned in dulcet tones.

She shook her head. "Never, Miss Luciana. I've seen you with that set expression on your face before, and never in twenty years have I known you to fail at what you set out to do when it came to something you really cared about. No, I have no doubt you'll get what you want. But I'll be mighty interested in how you set about doing it."

"I'll keep you informed," I promised, glancing at the ornate clock that was miraculously still in working order. Quarter past nine, and I still had to sneak up to the second floor and the cavernous closet where I remembered seeing an ancient mask and domino during our cleaning spree. I yawned hugely. "My, I'm exhausted. I can't imagine why I'm so tired all the time, Maggie. Aren't you tired, too?"

The look she cast me from her heavily fringed brown eyes was just slightly suspicious. "I've never known you to sleep so much in my entire life. Are you sure you're feeling all right, Miss Luciana?"

"Never been better," I said stoutly, simulating another yawn. "I'm just tired, that's all. Why don't we both go to bed early tonight and start the day at a more reasonable hour?"

"I think nine o'clock is a very reasonable hour to start the day," Maggie grumbled. "No one's up but milkmaids before then." She shook out the folds of the blue flowered dress. "Besides, I'd rather stay up and finish this. It does me no credit at all to see you wandering around Venice in those ugly old things." She cast a contemptuous eye over my tired old dress.

"Suit yourself," I said with an excellent show of unconcern, rising from the chaise longue and yawning once more. "I'll see you in the morning, then."

"Miss Luciana . . ." Maggie peered up at me. "You're up to something."

"Up to something? Why, Maggie, how absurd!" I laughed convincingly.

"I've known you all my life, Miss Luciana," she said in a sober voice. "And I know when you're up to something. And knowing you, it's bound to be dangerous. I just want you to know, Miss Luciana, that I've loved every moment I've spent with you."

"Humbug!" I said bracingly. "You didn't care at all for the time I ran off with the circus, nor for the time I tried to go on the stage. And I shall continue to lead you a merry dance for as long as you care to follow. It will take more than a pack of Venetian and Austrian scoundrels to make an end of me." I gave her a brisk, bone-cracking hug. "Good night, my dear. And don't worry about me."

"How can I help it?" she asked of the room in general. "I wish to God your father was here."

"To protect me?" I questioned.

"No," she grumbled. "To beat some sense into your idiotic skull."

CHAPTER EIGHT

It all proved far easier than I would have thought. The domino was right where I remembered it and was only slightly moth-eaten. My escape from Edentide was easily accomplished through the garden door, with no sound from the west salon to worry me about Maggie's surveillance. The gondolier looked vaguely familiar, and I wondered uneasily as I stepped into the gently rocking craft whether he had been dogging our footsteps during the entire last two days. As we pulled away from the quayside I saw a small, dark figure scuttle into the shadows, and suddenly I felt very small and very alone, surrounded by threatening creatures of the night. Surreptitiously I reached down and patted the huge kitchen knife I had secreted in one of my capacious pockets. Having willfully done away with what I assumed was Bones's protection, my hapless Uncle Mark, I would have to rely on myself alone. The thought was not overly reassuring.

We toured the back waterways at a leisurely

pace, and I willed myself to relax. A strange sort of yowl suddenly welled up from the stern of the boat, and I felt my skin crawl in horror. The yowl was followed by another, and then another, and with near hysterical relief I recognized it. It was neither an infant being strangled nor one of those infamous Venetian alley cats. My gondolier had decided to serenade me.

There was no way I could silence the ghastly sounds of his reedy, nasal tenor with the unfortunate tendency to aim a little high for his pitch. Gritting my teeth into a semblance of a smile, I leaned back among the shabby cushions and trailed a languid hand in the warm salt water. Surely we would reach Tonetti soon, and he would put a stop to this God-awful caterwauling.

I still held a trace of hope that Tonetti and the urgency of the situation would send all trace of Evan Fitzpatrick from my fickle mind. I had already an image of Tonetti: tall, broad shouldered with raven dark hair, a cynical, dashing smile on his mobile mouth, strong yet gentle hands, and a charmingly deferential, flattering manner. In looks he would be startlingly like an Italianate version of Evan Fitzpatrick, in manner completely opposite. I sighed, and then winced, as my gondolier started on a new aria.

"Saaaaaaantaaaaa Looooooooocheeeeeeyaaaaa,"

he howled, and my head began to pound. Just when I thought I could bear it no more, the gondola slowed, the voice mercifully stopped, and we pulled alongside a mooring pole outside an ancient pink palazzo, completely dark and deserted. As a matter of fact the entire waterway was devoid of people, and my skin began to prickle. It would be such an easy matter to dispose of an innocent, inquisitive young English lady. I watched the gondolier tie up to the mooring, once more trying to place the familiar shape of him.

When we were secure he turned and minced over to me, a difficult task in the rocking boat, and the fitful moonlight illuminated his face.

"You're the servant from the embassy!" I cried, in mingled relief and disappointment.

To my amazement he sank down on the cushions beside me, grabbed one hand in his soft, white ones, and pressed a very wet kiss upon it.

"Savior of Venice!" he declaimed thrillingly. "You see before you your humble slave, Enrico Tonetti! I am ready to lay down my life for you and the cause of a free Venice! I have only lived for this moment!"

Every word was vibrant with passion, and I stared at him with mingled amazement and distaste. "Mr. Tonetti . . . I . . ."

"No!" He held up one slim white hand, heavy laden with rings. The scent of lilac was strong about him—no, almost overwhelming—and it clashed badly with the Macassar oil that slicked down his thinning brown hair over an obvious bald spot. His eyes were brown and spaniellike and deliberately full of devotion, his mouth thick lipped and wet, his smile shy, ingratiating, and totally false. "You must call me Enrico, my sweet little pigeon. Or Tonetti, if you must. But none of this formal, English 'Mister' . . ." Once more he kissed my hand. "We are in this together, eh? Two agents with a duty to perform. For you, dear lady, I am . . ."

"Mr. Tonetti!" I snapped sternly, nettled. "I don't know why you are acting like this, but believe me there's no need. We are going to work together, not have an affair! If you would be so kind as to move back a bit . . . ?" Belatedly, he did so. "And if you could bring me up to date on the situation here in Venice. Have you any idea how I shall get into the general's rooms . . . ?"

Tonetti shrugged his thin shoulders sulkily. "I beg your pardon, dear lady. I cannot help it, it comes naturally to me. All my life I have adored the ladies. When I see a beautiful creature like yourself, all common sense is thrown to the winds.

I promise I won't forget myself again." And to prove it, he pinched me.

I responded by socking him in the jaw, and tears of pain and hurt sprang into his expressive dark eyes. I judged him to be somewhat past forty, with the vain hope that he appeared fifteen years younger. "I trust you to behave yourself, Tonetti!" I said, sounding like a schoolmarm. "I gather this business is new to the both of us. If we can't rely on each other, I don't doubt we'll be in a rare pickle."

"Ah, but you are one of the aristocracy," he complained in a gentle sort of whine. "Nothing will happen to you other than they will deport you and slap your pretty little wrist. Tonetti will be garroted." He made a nasty strangling noise in his throat, and I shivered.

"Then why are you taking such risks?"

He struck a pose, with one hand in the Venetian night and the other in the area of his heart. "For the glorious cause of a free and united Italy!" he cried.

"For the money," I corrected cynically.

"That, too," he agreed, dropping his hand swiftly. "What with the *dimostrazióne* keeping everyone out of Venice, it is hard for a man to make a living. And I have a wife and nine children to support."

"I am sure it is very difficult," I soothed. "What do you usually do? Are you a gondolier?"

He looked affronted. "Gondolier? Pah!" he spat into the canal. "Dear lady, do I look like a gondolier?" he demanded, and courtesy required me to assure him he did not. "When society is more normal, madonna, I am Venice's very finest gigolo."

It took me a moment to digest this casually offered information. "Doesn't your wife mind?" I choked out after a long moment.

"But why should she? She knows I am perfectly safe. It is all for looks, the bella figura, you know. What my sweet Maria doesn't like is when I don't bring home enough money, and then I must lower myself to more menial tasks, such as using my brother-in-law's gondola to bring in a few scudi." He sighed with the injustice of it all.

"But I thought your brother-in-law was General Eisenhopf's valet," I protested. "I thought that was how we were to gain admittance to his rooms. . . ."

"My dear lady, I have seven sisters. All of whom have husbands. It is my brother-in-law Federico who has the gondola. My brother-in-law Livio is the valet. And I don't wish to involve him if I can help it. He will only want a share of the money."

I could not fault the man for his candor. "Have you made any plans?" I brought him back to more important matters. "How in the world are we to accomplish this?"

"Dear lady, of course I have made plans!" he appeared affronted. "It is all very simple. Sometime this week General Eisenhopf will be out of town on a very secret mission. Only his valet knows of this, apparently. He is planning to leave in the early afternoon and tell no one. You will simply dress in your most becoming dress"—a small sneer accompanied his glance down at my bottle-green costume showing through the domino—"and walk right into his room. Many women have done so, it will not be remarked upon. Your Italian is the pure Venetian kind; there will be no suspicions. While you are there you will search the room, and once you have found the paper you will leave, telling the guard outside you were tired of waiting for the old pig. I will be right outside the barracks, ready to receive you and your paper. And I will then take you back to the palazzo, you will board the next train for England, and Venice will be saved!" His voice rose to theatrical heights once more, and the lilac perfume wafted over me.

"And when is all this to happen?" I inquired sweetly.

"I will have to let you know." He lost some of his bravado. "I have not yet ascertained when it is that the general is leaving. Perhaps if you could meet me in the Piazza tomorrow, I may have some word for you. But believe me, dear lady, there will be no danger to you whatsoever. It is I, Tonetti, who takes all the risks, and you who shall reap all the glory!" The nobility of this left him much moved.

"And you, Tonetti, will also have all the money," I remarked caustically. "That should comfort you on your long, gloryless nights."

"My nights, dear lady, are always filled with glory. You need only ask my wife." He drew himself up with full dignity.

"I am sure they are. I have not yet spoken of you to my Uncle Mark. I felt he would only complicate matters."

"Very wise, signorina. And what of that sweet little bambina who follows you everywhere?" He kissed his hands expressively.

"She is not to know anything either. The fewer people who know of this, the better. I doubt that either of them would be much good in a crisis."

"Then it is just the two of us, dear lady!" Once more he tried to embrace me, but a sharp elbow in his ribs dissuaded him.

"Just the two of us, Tonetti," I agreed, my heart sinking with a sudden, awful foreboding. "God help us."

CHAPTER NINE

"For Gawd's sake, slow down, Miss Luciana!" Maggie panted behind me, scuttling gracelessly over the cobbled bridge that spanned the small canal. "Why are we in such a hurry?"

Abruptly I stopped, and Maggie crashed into me, my tall, strong body absorbing the blow with no trouble. Holding up the leather and gold cover of my book, I adorned my face with an idiotic simper for the edification of all around on the crowded thoroughfare, both Venetian and Austrian.

"Maggie, dear, I haven't done any sightseeing. And Mr. Ruskin's book is sooo fascinating," I cooed. "If only I could understand him a little better." Pouting prettily, I batted my eyes at a passing Tedesco who smirked in response, his thick Austrian lips curving in a leer. I dropped my voice so that no one else could hear. "Besides, I expect things to come to a head quite swiftly. If I'm to see anything at all of Venice before I leave, I'd better hurry."

The Demon Count's Daughter

If the prospect of our imminent departure didn't fill me with overwhelming pleasure, it was not to be wondered at. I had barely spoken two words to Evan Fitzpatrick, and how I would remedy that situation in the time allotted me was beyond imagining. My first duty was to Venice and Tonetti, but I knew in the question of Evan I would have to move fast. If I didn't secure his attention here in Venice, I might as well give up hope. In stately England the man wouldn't be allowed in the same county as me. I quickened my steps.

"If you fall, Miss Luciana, and soil your new dress," Maggie threatened, panting beside me, "I personally will push you in a canal. Right in front of a gondola."

I looked down with pleasure at the blue-and-white-flowered cotton dress swirling about my blue leather shoes. "Maggie, I'll guard it with my life," I swore, smugly aware of how attractive I was. Before I had time to congratulate myself too warmly, we were upon the Piazza with the golden-domed, ornate splendor of St. Mark's and the Doges' Palace ahead of us.

"Will you look at that," Maggie breathed. "Is that where we're going?" She thrust one ripe hip forward to catch the attention of a handsome young gondolier.

I nodded. "It is indeed. We'll start with the

basilica, then perhaps climb the Campanile, then the clock tower, and then the Doges' Palace. And after that we'll stop at Florian's Café for sugar and water." Tonetti, in parting, hadn't said where or when he would meet us. All of Venice eventually ended up in the Piazza, and I intended to partake of its myriad treats fully, leaving it up to the perfumed gigolo to find me.

"What a treat," Maggie said with less enthusiasm. "Why don't we start with the church, then the palace (I do so love palaces), and see how our energy holds out. I've been staying up late sewing for you, miss. I'm tired!" she yawned convincingly, winking unabashedly at the now-staring Venetian.

"Well, you can sit at Florian's and drink coffee while I continue exploring," I agreed with a show of reluctance. "But I'm sure you'd be missing a great pleasure."

"Pleasures like that I can afford to miss every now and then, Miss Luciana. Let's start with the church."

In a way I could understand Maggie's boredom. St. Mark's was gloriously ornate, the mosaics glowing with color, the golden altar, bronze doors, marble columns, all contributing to an aura of somehow pagan splendor that wasn't much in keeping with my image of the holy mother church. This was the heart and soul of Venice, and yet somehow I wondered if it were the heart and soul of Luciana Carlotta del Zaglia. I had always assumed it was, but now suddenly I was having doubts.

"What does Mr. Ruskin say about this?" Maggie questioned in somewhat strident tones, pointing to a glorious mosaic of Salome in a stunning red medieval dress, dancing with lascivious abandon with John the Baptist's head borne aloft above her typically Venetian blond plaits.

"Not much," I replied, leafing through the tedious little book. "But she is magnificent, isn't she?" I stared up at her in profound admiration. "That's what I'd like to be like," I sighed longingly. "Bold and beautiful and seductive and powerful."

"I would say you've got a fair start," she remarked pertly. "I only hope you don't have men who scorn you decapitated."

I laughed. "A fitting punishment. I can't say as I blame the woman."

"Let's try the Doges' Palace," Maggie sighed after a moment, "and then we might go for some coffee. The café on the left as we came in seemed very pleasant."

"Maggie!" I murmured, shocked. "That was the

Quadri. It's patronized by the Austrians and their sympathizers. Never the Venetians!"

"But Miss Luciana, you aren't Venetian either. You're three-quarters English, and there's no way you can change that."

I opened my mouth to protest, then shut it again. The simple truth was inescapable. "Well, even if I have a great deal of chilly English blood," I snapped, "it doesn't mean that I have to approve of the Tedeschi."

"Especially not with your parentage, Miss del Zaglia," a smooth Austrian voice broke through as we stepped into the dazzling sunlight, and it was all I could do to turn a bland, polite face to Holger von Wolfram.

"How nice to see you again, Colonel," I murmured calmly, batting my eyelashes in a manner that left the Austrian entirely unmoved. "My disapproval of the Imperial Army doesn't necessarily have to extend to individuals."

He bowed with perfect gallantry at my flirtatious remark. "I would hope not, Fräulein. Each of us has our duty to perform, no matter how unpleasant we may find it, but we must only hope that one can somehow remain friends."

A small chill ran down my spine. "And what unpleasant duties have you to perform, Colonel?"

He smiled, and the chill deepened. "But I was

speaking of yourself, dear Fräulein. Have you seen the Ducal Palace? You must be sure not to miss it before you return to England. Which I trust will be soon. For your sake, as well as that of others."

I gave him a smile to match the dazzling brilliance of the Venetian sunlight. "I will see the Ducal Palace very soon, Colonel. In a matter of minutes, in fact. And I will be sure to pass on to my friends at home everything I see and hear while I'm in this glorious *Italian* city."

"You willfully misunderstand me," he growled. "Your parents did not warn you about me."

"Oh, yes, they did," I corrected him cheerfully. "But I choose not to be intimidated by an aging toy soldier." Nodding my head regally, I swept by him, with a nervous Maggie in my wake.

"Should you have been so rude, Miss Luciana?" she demanded, horrified, as we strode across the Piazza toward the Ducal Palace with well-disguised haste. "He seems a powerful enemy to make."

"I didn't just make him my enemy," I turned and said coldly, still shaken from the encounter. "He's been my enemy since long before I was born. I no longer care who knows it." I started forward again. "Come along, Maggie."

A loud groan answered me, and I whirled back to find my maid clutching her ankle, an expression of agonizing pain on her suddenly pale face. "Maggie, what's wrong?" I demanded.

"A stone in my shoe, Miss Luciana. I think I'd best go back home. You go on ahead without me; I'll be fine." She took a few hobbling steps.

"I'll do no such thing. The Doges' Palace has been here for centuries, it will last a bit longer. I'll go get help." Briefly I thought of Tonetti, and abandoned the idea as hopeless.

"Don't be an idiot," my polite maid whispered sharply. "Go on ahead to the palace. A certain gentleman has been watching us from the portico, obviously awaiting us. It won't do you any good to have your chaperon trailing around after you." I looked up sharply, expecting to see Tonetti. Instead, Evan Fitzpatrick's tall form disappeared into the palace just ahead of us.

"But Maggie, your foot . . ." I protested weakly.

"There's nothing wrong with my damned foot," she hissed. "Go on ahead. I'll go back over the Rialto Bridge and get you a bolt of nice, soft muslin. In a warm, butter yellow, I think." And she hobbled off with amazing speed, leaving me staring after her with mingled amusement and fear. And absolute amazement that wherever I happened to go in this city of water I would always run into Evan Fitzpatrick. It must be fate, or God's will, or something equally nebulous. And there was nothing I could do but stifle my conscience and give in to that fate. Tonetti and the future of Venice could wait another afternoon.

There was no sign of him when I entered the Ducal Palace. Throwing back my shoulders, I started forward.

I found him all alone in the square drawing room at the top of the great golden staircase, staring up with seemingly rapt attention at the ceiling painting, which my guidebook informed me was by Tintoretto, entitled "Doge G. Pruili with Justice, Peace, and St. Jerome." If I hadn't known better, I would have thought the Englishman had been following me, rather than the other way around. The room was deserted but for the two of us, and, after casting only a cursory glance at the florid masterpiece above my head, I cleared my throat alarmingly.

His extraordinary blue eyes swept over me in complete unconcern and then went back to their perusal of the ceiling. Undaunted, I took in all the glorious details of him—a far more impressive work of art as far as I was concerned.

He was so delightfully tall I could scarce believe it after a lifetime of being surrounded by short men. I knew from experience that he topped me by a good three inches, and that, coupled with his broad, strong shoulders, which stretched the black careless coat he wore with such a dash, was enough to make any young girl swoon. His legs were long and well muscled, his ungloved hands both strong and sensitive-looking. The dark blond hair fell away from his face as he looked upward, his strong nose and chin in profile, the scar away from me. With great determination I dropped Mr. Ruskin on the floor with a loud thump, consigning Tonetti and his plots to a temporary perdition.

Once more he turned from his endless admiration of the tedious work of art, his eyes sweeping from my book on the marble floor, to my face, to the floor once more. A cynical smile curved his lips, and he moved with pantherish grace to retrieve the fallen Mr. Ruskin.

He would have turned away without a word if I hadn't quickly spoken. "It's a very boring book, you know."

He halted, reluctantly. "Is it?" he sounded very bored himself.

"Yes, it is," I pushed on. "I came to one sentence that had two hundred and thirty-five words in it. Truly! I counted every one."

Some of the mockery faded from the smile, leaving genuine amusement, a much more attractive emotion. "I have no doubt that you did. If you will excuse me, Miss . . ." He started to go, but once more I detained him.

"You knew my name two days ago."

The brief smile was chilly now. "Did I? Well, I have since forgotten it."

This time I did hold out my slender, gloved hand. "Then I shall have to remind you. My name is Luciana Carlotta del Zaglia."

He continued to stare down at me, making no attempt to take my hand, no attempt to introduce himself. I could feel my face flushing beneath his cool, aloof regard. "And your name is Evan Fitzpatrick," I pushed on.

"I can thank Lady Bute for that, I suppose," he said coolly. "My dear Miss del Zaglia, I would suggest you refrain from accosting strange men in your peregrinations over Venice. Despite Lady Bute's assertions, I am a gentleman, but the next man your wayward fancy lights upon might not be one. Good day to you." And he turned that lovely, broad back on me and strode out the door, leaving me gasping with hurt, indignation, and rage.

Before I had time to master my conflicting emotions, one of the side doors opened and two surprisingly rough-looking Venetians entered. I peered at them closely, but neither was my absent gigolo. As I watched them move into the room, I thought absently how sweet it was that the lowest of Venetians would still be interested in their local treasures, the other part of me still envisioning Evan Fitzpatrick's head on a plate with me in a red dress like the mosaic Salome's, when suddenly I realized that the two brigands were not looking at the ceiling. They were looking straight at me and moving toward me with a great show of determination, something that looked ominously like a rope and a sack in their filthy hands. "That's the girl," the first one muttered. "It should be simple enough."

I darted to one side, but they were too fast for me. One meaty hand grabbed my wrist, while another cuffed me across the face with a force that stunned me, but only momentarily. A moment later I was down on the hard, marble floor kicking, biting, and scratching, my tormentors rather ineptly trying to control a giant madwoman as she fought tooth and nail.

One of the creatures kept trying to force a filthy rag into my mouth, and I barely had time to scream for help before I felt myself choking. A knife flashed, and I grew still, knowing my furious strength could do little good against that shining blade.

"That is very good," one of the men chuckled, his mouth showing stained and broken teeth. "The English lady will keep her mouth full of that, won't she? No more screams for this 'Evan,' eh?"

He yanked me to my feet and began binding

me roughly with the thick hemp rope. The sack he held in one dirty hand was a capacious one, but not made for my noble proportions, and he tossed it in one corner with a curse. "We'll have to take her out the back way, Gianni," he muttered. "The Tedeschi want her alive."

"I don't think you will." A dry, English voice broke through, and the three of us turned in amazement to see Evan Fitzpatrick standing very coolly in the doorway.

They hadn't had time to secure my bonds, and after a short struggle I slipped them off as my two abductors began circling round, edging toward Evan with murder on their swarthy, villainous faces. Yanking the rag out of my mouth, I spat a few times and then commenced screaming at the top of my rather powerful lungs.

Gianni turned back to me, rage and confusion on his bovine face. The knife flashed, and I felt the sleeve of my dress rip, followed by a trail of wet, warm blood down my arm. My first thought was of Maggie's rage at the destruction of her newest creation, and then I realized the danger in which both Evan and I stood.

"Goddamn it, Lucy, run!" Evan shouted, as the other villain jumped on him, and for a moment the two of them were a hideous, frightening tangle of thrashing limbs, the knife gleaming as they rolled around the floor. Gianni stared, unable to decide who to stab first, me or the Englishman, and I took advantage of his indecision to fling the heavy rope in his face.

It was like a red flag in front of an angry bull. I heard a hideous grunt behind me, but I had no chance to see who was the victor. I began backing away from the Italian, slowly, and he followed me just as slowly, an incredibly evil grin on his heretofore simple face. And then, horribly, I felt the solid marble wall behind me and knew I could escape no farther. I shut my eyes and prepared to meet my death.

Another hideous grunt followed, and I opened my eyes once more to watch Evan grappling with him, a cold, murderous expression on his face, which was even more frightening than the simple malice of my abductors. Loud noises and running feet came from the corridor. "Avanti, Gianni," the first man shouted as he struggled to his feet. With a sudden burst of strength the second man flung Evan aside, and I saw the knife flash. And then they were gone, leaving their two wounded victims.

I met Evan's eyes across the room. He was panting, disheveled, and blood oozed from a cut high up on his thigh. I could feel my hair slipping from its pins, and the wetness at my fingertips told me my own wound was bleeding in a cheerfully profuse manner.

Limping slightly, he moved across the floor and retrieved the shawl I had dropped during the melee. "Wrap this around you," he ordered tersely, holding it out to me.

Numbly I did as I was told, my eyes never leaving his pale, sweat-streaked face. We could hear voices from a great distance heading our way, and without another word he grabbed my good arm, his touch surprising me with its magnetic effect.

"Let's get the hell out of here," he muttered, dragging me forward out the door down the glorious wide, golden stairway, our mingled blood leaving small patches on the floor.

"But shouldn't we report this?" I demanded breathlessly, feeling stupidly weak.

"To Holger von Wolfram?" He questioned cynically. "I think not. Who do you think hired them? Those two men are known to be Austrian hirelings. How bad is your arm?" His voice held a rough concern that made me bless my shallow wound.

"Only a scratch, I think. And your leg?"

He smiled down at me wryly, and I was in love. "It'll do. Can you manage to walk a ways?"

"I think so." Holding on to him like this, I was

fully capable of walking miles. "Where are we going?"

"To my flat. Since you're so anxious to compromise yourself, that should please you no end."

I was about to flare up at him when I saw a wince of pain flash momentarily in his beautiful eyes. And I knew he would never make it to his quarters alone. I summoned up my best smile, held on to him a little more tightly, and said nothing, smiling like the Giorgione Madonna Maggie had likened me to. And if there was a touch of Salome in me, how was anyone else to know?

CHAPTER TEN

I have never had so long or so nerve-racking a walk. Blindly I followed where Evan led, knowing by the inexorable strength of his muscles that he must be in great pain, but his face was smooth and expressionless. I draped my shawl around my arm, allowing it to trail down so that it hung and obscured his wound.

Down the wide, tourist-filled expanse of the Piazza San Marco, down narrow alleys, past churches and small canals and shops and palazzos, I walked until I thought I should faint with the tension and the heat. And suddenly the La Fenice Theatre loomed up in front of us, and Evan's feet finally slowed their relentless pace until we came to a small, neat, pink building with window boxes brimming with nasturtiums of a riotously clashing orange and red.

"You'll have to keep your voice down," he warned me, his face still blank. The only inkling I had of the strain he was under was the unnatural paleness of his face, paleness that touched everywhere but the thin, red line of his scar. "My landlady is a very strict widow who doesn't approve of ladies in gentlemen's rooms."

I nodded, following him silently up the narrow, twisting stairs. It was as well he had warned me; it was all I could do not to cry out as his customary grace deserted him for a moment and he stumbled against the wall. Hastily he pulled himself upright, leaving a dark red splotch of blood on the whitewashed surface.

Vainly I tried to scrub at the mark with my now blood-soaked shawl, but it only served to smear it. "Leave it," he ordered briefly, and continued upward. There was nothing I could do but follow.

It was dark in the apartment, but blessedly cool after the burning heat of the midday sun. I stayed just inside the closed door, leaning against the wall and willing my cursed dizziness to pass. Such feminine weakness was not at all like me, and I could have wished for a better time for this sudden upsurge of delicacy. I took a few deep breaths, determined not to swoon, when I felt myself caught up in a pair of strong arms. The sensation was so pleasant I gave up all idea of fainting. And then the darkness closed in.

When consciousness returned I was lying stretched out on an exceedingly comfortable sofa;

Evan was beside me, bending over my arm and cleaning the long, deep scratch with assiduous care.

"Damn!" I said loudly and clearly, and those silver-blue eyes met mine for a startled moment.

"Damn what?"

"I have never fainted in my entire life," I assured him ruefully. "I certainly picked a fine time to do so."

"Never fainted?" he mocked. "How can any properly brought up young girl of these times and fashions say such a thing?" His voice was rough but his hands, as they carefully washed my wound, were incredibly gentle.

"I've never worn a corset," I explained reasonably. "Most women swoon because of tight lacing."

The look from those eyes was definitely perplexed, and too late I realized the impropriety of my words.

"Oh, damn," I said again. "I shouldn't have mentioned corsets, should I?"

"Certainly not. You also shouldn't say 'damn' so frequently," he said calmly, wrapping my arm in clean, soft linen. "What would your parents say if they heard you?"

I chortled. "They'd probably say, 'Damn it, don't swear so much.'" I eyed his handiwork with professional approval. "You do seem to take an inordinate amount of interest in my parents," I observed casually.

He leaned back on his heels, wincing slightly. "It fascinates me that they would let such an unprincipled hoyden as yourself loose upon Europe. I think a few years in a convent would do you a world of good." He rose abruptly, swaying imperceptibly, and a moment later I was on my feet.

"Sit down and let me see your wound," I ordered sternly, staring up into his scarred face with a determined expression.

"Certainly not," he snapped, manlike. "I'm entirely capable of taking care of it myself."

"Don't be absurd," I snapped back. "I have a great deal of experience in medical matters. I used to assist the village doctor in all manner of things. I've helped babies being born, amputations, typhus . . ."

"Then a mere knife wound should be too trivial for one of your vast experience. Unless you were planning on amputating."

"Evan," I said in a low, dangerous, not-to-be-thwarted tone of voice, "I must insist that you take off your pants and let me take care of your wound."

My voice trailed off before his burst of laughter. "You certainly are direct and to the point, aren't you?" he said after a moment. "Well, my dear child, if you have no modesty, I'm afraid I do." He limped over to a chair, lowering himself gingerly, and with the aid of strong fingers and a letter opener proceeded to rip away the remainder of his pants leg.

It was a great deal worse than I had expected, and as I knelt there on the floor, holding a wet compress to his thigh, I wondered that he had been able to walk so far with what had appeared to be only mild discomfort. "This must hurt you," I muttered under my breath as I tried to clean up the wound.

"Thank you, it does," he replied politely, watching me out of hooded eyes as I knelt between his long legs and worked on his wound. "You'll have to disinfect it," he said after a moment.

"I know that, much as I dislike the thought. Do you have any whiskey here?"

"Would an English gentleman's home be complete without a bottle of whiskey?" he mocked. "Over by the table." As I came back and knelt once more in front of him, some devil prompted him to tease me. "I do hope you're enjoying this, Lucy. Lady Bute will be dying to hear all the details of your encounter with the evil divorcé."

Calmly I poured whiskey all over the deep wound, wickedly pleased to see him stiffen in pain. "I have no intention of confiding this afternoon's adventures to Lady Bute. Perhaps I should tell you that you are not of such all-consuming interest to me as you seem to believe."

"Should you tell me that?" he said in an odd tone of voice.

I looked up and met his silver-blue eyes with a clear gaze. "Of course, I should. But it would be a lie." And with a splendid show of unconcern I went back to my task, wrapping the strips of linen around his lean, muscled thigh with only the slightest shaking of my hands, and I controlled my desperate urge to throw my arms around his waist and rest my head against his broad chest with more than average effort. When it was done I looked up again, surprising an odd expression on his face, one that I couldn't read at all.

"I've done my best," I said briskly. "It's my professional opinion that you should stay off it for the next few days."

"Is it now? And who's going to wait upon me, bring me my dinner, pour me my whiskey?" he questioned softly. "Were you planning to volunteer?"

Shaking my head, I rose abruptly and walked halfway across the room. His proximity had been even more disturbing than I had let myself realize. "I could do with a cup of tea," I said in a strangled tone of voice after a long moment. "Would you care for some?"

He nodded, pulling himself to his feet. "You'll find everything you need in the kitchen. In the meantime I'll change my clothes. And no"—he held up a restraining hand as I impulsively moved forward—"you may not help me. I am still entirely capable of taking off my clothes without your assistance. When I've changed and the tea is ready, my dear Lucy, I will be ready for your explanation." His eyes were like blue smoke. "And I expect it to be believable."

I found myself singing as I bustled around his kitchen, happier than I remembered being in a long, long time, despite the throb in my arm and the worry in my mind. I couldn't betray my business here in Venice—Bones would kill me. The more people who knew of my mission, the less chance of success. But oh, I did so want to confide in him!

I made the tea strong and peaty, a noble restorative, and carried it into the drawing room just as Evan emerged from the far doorway, dressed in a pair of soft brown pants and shirt sleeves. As I stared at him in witless admiration, I thought once again how very attractive men were in their loose white shirts, the collars unbuttoned to show the beginnings of a tanned throat. He moved across the room with the barest trace of a limp and took the tray from my nerveless fingers. And unbidden, the thought flashed through my mind that he must be accustomed to wounds far worse than his recent one to be able to survive it without more than a show of discomfort.

I poured for the two of us, suddenly shy, and silently allowed him to tip a generous dollop of whiskey into my tea cup. He leaned back on the sofa, took a deep drink of his spiked tea, and stared at me for a long, uneasy moment out of those hypnotizing eyes.

I cleared my throat. "I suppose you're wondering why those two . . . two men tried to hurt me," I said in what I hoped was a casual tone of voice. "You said they were Austrian hirelings?"

"That's exactly what they were. Now what has a sweet, innocent young lady like yourself done to earn the enmity of the Imperial Army?"

His casual words brought the unpleasant truth home to me with full force. Someone, some fairly powerful member of the Austrian forces, knew why I was here in Venice. My chances for success had just dropped to a bare possibility. I fiddled with my teacup, playing for time. "I suppose it might be because of my parents," I offered. "My father was a Venetian patriot—he made a lot of enemies twenty-five years ago." I sighed. "But why don't they just deport me? Why try to hurt me?"

"They were trying to kidnap you, my dear Lucy," he contradicted flatly. "Obviously they are under the impression you know something you shouldn't. Is that true?"

I gave him my most innocent, amber gaze, willing him to believe me. "What could I know?"

But Evan wasn't convinced. "That's for you to say. And they probably haven't got enough proof to deport you. Just suspicions, no doubt because of your family connections." His voice was lightly mocking. "When they can do nothing through normal channels it is a simple enough matter to dispatch two brigands to take care of things, no questions asked. I would suggest, my dear Lucy, that you keep away from dark alleys."

"Why do you call me Lucy?" I questioned out of the blue.

He raised an eyebrow. "Your name is Luciana, is it not? Lucy suits you better. Besides, I have no intention of trying to twist my tongue around your absurd name. I'll call you Lucy if I please."

"I wasn't objecting," I said evenly, meeting his gaze. "I'll do my best to keep out of solitary places from now on, I promise. Tell me," I hesitated a moment—"would you have killed them if they hadn't run away?" The thought had been preying on my mind for the last few minutes.

"Without a doubt." No remorse crossed his face, and I wondered at his callous attitude.

"You don't seem to mind the idea," I said crossly. "Have you killed men before?"

"I was a soldier, dear Lucy. I have killed a great many men in my life," he said wearily.

"And why are you no longer a soldier?"

He smiled, but it wasn't a pleasant smile. "I resigned my commission when I divorced my wife. Surely Lady Bute informed you of that juicy tidbit?"

"Why did you do that?" I asked with my usual subtlety and tact.

But Evan seemed disposed to enlighten me. "Why did I divorce my wife or why did I resign my commission?" There was a bleak, haunted look somewhere in the back of his eyes. "I divorced my wife rather than murder her. I resigned my commission rather than be cashiered. I was in a very old, very historic regiment that had no room for a divorced man in its noble ranks." His voice was flat and cold. "Which brings me back to you. I am waiting for your explanation."

"Explanation?" I echoed, confused. "I thought we agreed that they were two Austrian hirelings."

"Not about that, my angel," and the endearment

was mocking. "I want to know why you've been following me. Falling at my feet, tossing tea trays over young ladies, dropping books right and left. You don't do this with every man you meet, do you?" His voice was cool and clipped and so offensive I wanted to throw my teacup at his dark gold head. Instead I took another deep gulp, feeling the whiskey warm my bones and relax my tight nerves.

My, my, but he was an unhappy man! I would have gladly given ten years off my life to be able to go up to him and smooth away that angry, bitter expression from his handsome face, to press my lips against that angry red scar. And as quickly as it had come all my fury evaporated. "Not every man," I replied lightly. "Only the most attractive."

"Hasn't that gotten you into a great deal of trouble?" he barked. "How many men has your fancy lighted upon?"

I smiled sweetly. "Only one."

A long silence ensued. "Well, then, my dear Lucy, I suggest you take yourself back to England as soon as possible and see if you can find some other young man to take your fancy. If I'm the first man you've been attracted to, then you can't be long out of the schoolroom. Go back to England

and your parents can introduce you to some likely young men."

I finished the tea, poured myself some more, and added a generous dose of whiskey. "I am twenty-three years old, Evan," I said calmly. "I have had a season, met scores of eligible young men, received three proposals of marriage, two of which were fairly suitable."

"Then why didn't you accept them?"

I took a deep breath and plunged right in there. "Because for the last twenty-three years I've been waiting for you."

The next pause was even longer. His teacup crashed down on the tray. "Jesus Christ!" he swore. "You must be completely out of your mind!"

To my relief I could recognize the strange blend of irritation, amusement, and fascination in his angry eyes, and I continued with more assurance. "Not at all. And you, my dearest Evan, have been waiting for me for the last . . . thirty-six years?"

"Thirty-seven," he corrected absently. "Which goes to prove that I'm too old for you anyway. I doubt my dear Amelia would have agreed that I'd been waiting for you."

"Well," I said with great practicality, "from what I hear of your late wife, you would have been a lot better off waiting for me, instead of getting involved with a monster like that."

He rose then and stalked across the room, looking more and more like the dangerous panther I had likened him to. He leaned over my chair, putting his hands on the arms and effectively imprisoning me. His face was very close, and his blue eyes blazed in a rage of noble proportions.

"My dear Lucy," he said softly, dangerously, "you are playing with fire. You cannot come to a man's apartment and tell him that you've been waiting for him all your life and then expect nothing to happen. Especially when you're absurdly lovely."

I met his gaze serenely. "What *is* going to happen?"

He stood up abruptly, yanking me to my feet with a jerk that left my arm throbbing more than ever. "Just this," he said in an undertone, and brought his mouth down on mine.

I had never been kissed like that before, either in love or in anger, and it was quite a devastating experience. He forced my mouth open with his, and his tongue plundered me ruthlessly, a cruel invader with no love, tenderness, or affection. Instinctively I resisted the harshness of his embrace, but it only served to increase his determination. My mouth was bruised, I could taste blood from my lip mixed with the whiskey on his breath, and still he kissed me, his hands like iron bars around me, so that I couldn't break free. And then suddenly I didn't want to escape. Twining my arms around his neck I wove my fingers through his long, fair curls and answered his mouth as completely as my inexperience and infatuation allowed. And the violence left him, his lips softened on mine, moving to my eyes, my cheeks, my forehead in short, sweet, unhurried little kisses. A small sigh of pleasure escaped me as he brought his mouth to mine once more, and then suddenly I was thrust away, alone and lost, with the shelter of his arms brutally withdrawn.

Turning his back on me, he strode across to the chaise longue, retrieved my blood-stained shawl, and tossed it to me with an abrupt gesture. "Wrap this around you," he ordered coldly, "and I'll see you home."

It was just slightly more than I could take. "Coward," I said clearly and distinctly, and ran from the room, not bothering to shut the door behind me. A moment later I was lost in the crowded alleys, as all of Venice headed toward their afternoon promenade along St. Mark's Square, and, to my despair, there was no tall shadow behind me.

CHAPTER ELEVEN

There was no way I could hide my damaged condition from my ever-faithful Maggie. With questions, shrieks of outrage, solicitous care, and stern scoldings she divested me of my blue flowered dress, which she swore she could salvage, brewed some strong, whiskeyless tea, and tucked me up in bed with a nice custard as a restorative and a box of rich, creamy chocolates.

"Where did the candy come from?" I demanded as I settled back among the feather pillows, my eyes devouring the luscious chocolates that my tea and whiskey-filled stomach rejected.

"They were delivered a short while before you got home," Maggie replied, distracted. "I couldn't find a note."

"Probably lost during delivery," I said easily. "Maggie, dear, could I . . . ?" I held up my empty bowl appealingly, and a moment later I was alone.

The note wasn't too difficult to find, if you knew where to look. At this point I was getting used to

Tonetti's flowery style, though the lilac scent ruined two perfectly good chocolates.

"Beloved Angel," it read, and mournfully I remembered who else had called me angel that day. "Words cannot describe my feelings of despair at missing you this afternoon! Only say that your poor, wretched servant may hope to see you tomorrow. Otherwise, all will be lost! Your slave, Enrico Tonetti."

I crumpled the note in my hand, wishing desperately that I had someone to turn to other than that scented fop, someone to confide in. There was little doubt in my mind who I wanted that someone to be, and unbidden, the feel of his mouth on mine returned with shattering force. Wearily I crawled deeper under the covers, huddling against the damp, the loneliness, and the danger of the Venice night.

It took all my powers of persuasion and native guile to escape Maggie's almost fanatical surveillance the next afternoon. All morning she had clung to me like a limpet, devising the most absurdly obvious reasons for me not to leave the moldering palazzo. For the time being I was only too happy to stay within the ancient walls of the family home. Despite the centuries of violence that had abounded in and around the old palace, there was a curious aura of peace and serenity which

I found most appealing. I knew full well that I hadn't much time for peace and serenity left to me in Venice. Obviously Tonetti's plans had been made. It was up to me to prepare myself, both physically and mentally, for the ordeal ahead. And the first thing I had to do was put Evan Fitzpatrick firmly out of my mind.

But that was easier said than done. Dutifully I sat in a small, hard chair in the west salon and stitched with careful little stitches on Maggie's newest creation, a muslin frock of butter yellow that would undoubtedly make me look like an overgrown daffodil. I could think of worse things to look like. And instead of Tonetti, all morning long my mind kept going back to Evan Fitzpatrick and the feel of his mouth on mine, his hard, clever hands caressing my love-starved body with a sureness that came from long and diligent practice.

It wasn't the first time I had ever been kissed. Various proper young gentlemen had pressed importunate, dry lips against mine during indiscreet evening walks. One had even gone so far as to tumble me into a sheltering clump of bushes. The poor young viscount had returned to the party with a blackened eye and severely impaired dignity, and I, my virtue still intact. But nothing had prepared me for the sudden upsurge of passion, the simple, immediate desire that had swept over me yesterday when Evan had touched me. And I remembered vaguely my thought then, that, of course, this is how it should be.

"Whatever it is you're thinking of," Maggie broke in caustically, "you'd better get down on your knees and pray for forgiveness. I've never seen so wanton a look on anyone's face in my life."

Quickly I pulled myself back together. "Then you've never looked in a mirror," I shot back, pleased with my sally. "I have no reason to pray for forgiveness, Maggie. I was just daydreaming."

"That was more than daydreaming, Miss Luciana. There's some practical knowledge in your eyes that wasn't there before, or I miss my guess. I don't know what your parents will say." She sighed gustily.

Carefully I knotted the thread. "They will say, Maggie, that it's about time." I put the froth of yellow material to one side. "And now I think I'll take a nap. I haven't been getting enough sleep since we've been in Venice." I yawned convincingly.

Suspicion flared in her mild hazel eyes. "You've never needed more than a few hours' sleep before, Miss Luciana. Why are you so tired all of the time?"

"I think all this heat enervates me," I replied

guilelessly. "Why don't you take a nap yourself, Maggie? It's too hot to do anything else."

She looked torn, and the moment she spoke I realized her dilemma. Lust and duty had always been stern taskmasters, and she was leaning heavily in the former, having devoted her morning to her hapless charge. "There's a very nice young man who's offered to take me for a ride in his boat," she said with what in another person I might have called shyness. "If you really don't need me I might let him know that I'd be available this afternoon. . . ."

"I'm sure he already knows that you're available, Maggie," I murmured, eyeing her low-cut dress that pulled across her straining bodice. In anyone else I might have thought the dress needed alteration, but with Maggie I knew it had been designed with that effect carefully in mind. "You go on ahead. I think I might explore some of the upper rooms, maybe nap up there. There might be more of a breeze up near the top floor." I waved a hand listlessly in front of my face, stirring the warm, humid air only slightly.

Poor Maggie still hesitated. "Well, if you're sure. I'd be glad to stay, Miss Luciana, if you thought it would be necessary. Pietro could come another day."

"Maggie, I shall be sound asleep in five minutes,

and no doubt will sleep till dinnertime." I yawned again, hoping to hide the tense excitement that stirred beneath my uncorseted breast. "Don't waste another moment on me, for heaven's sake."

"Well, if you're sure . . ." she agreed doubtfully. "I only hope I can trust you to do as you say, and not leave the house."

I looked shocked and hurt. "Maggie, would I lie to you?" I protested. Maggie only shook her head.

It took me five minutes to change into the newly mended blue flowered dress with its shorter, modified sleeves, repin my long, thick hair, and find a fresh pair of gloves before I was out the door. I had no idea what time Tonetti planned to find me, but I knew I should make myself available for as long a time as possible. Maggie would come looking for me by five, but it was only half-past two, and I could take my time.

By their own accord my feet started toward the Merceria and the Rialto Bridge. I wandered among the shops, most of them closed in the broiling early afternoon sun, and bought a few things: some bright yellow ribbons to match my dress, an ell of lace, which would look exquisite with my mother's light coloring, a string of millefiori beads that were far too expensive.

In Italy all roads lead to Rome. In Venice all streets and canals seem to lead inexorably to St. Mark's Square. It wasn't long before I found myself strolling along the pavement stones on the huge square, peering into shop windows, ignoring the milling Austrian soldiers in their gaudy uniforms and loud cheeriness.

St. Mark's Square seemed like an odd choice for a meeting, overflowing as it was with boisterous Austrians, curious Englishmen, superior Frenchmen, all of whom eyed me with embarrassing approval.

One ruddy-faced young soldier had just left his seat at one of the cafés and headed toward me when I saw Tonetti off to one side, resplendent in a pale lavender suit, beckoning me. When the Austrian looked again, I had disappeared under the New Procuratie, strolling along with seeming abandon as I chatted with my Venetian lover.

"Signorina del Zaglia," he breathed, his spaniel's eyes moist with passion and a darting look of fear. "I have been half-crazy with worry." He seized my gloved hand and began slobbering over it, dampening the thin kid. I forced myself to bestow a flirtatious smile upon his oiled and thinning hair.

"For heaven's sake, control yourself," I hissed,

snatching back my hand with a fond glance. "Don't overdo the whole thing."

He pressed one well-manicured hand to his breast. "Forgive me, Madonna," he said soulfully. "But the loveliness of your radiant graciousness makes me forget myself. Ah, if this were only a dream; the two of us could go off together, away from all this . . ."

"On whose money?" I questioned cruelly. "All English ladies are not heiresses, you know."

"But . . . but you are a del Zaglia!" he protested, momentarily disconcerted. "Of course you have money."

"Only if my parents approve," I informed him. "Besides, I don't think your wife and nine children would care for it."

"Soon to be ten," he corrected glumly. "My wife informed me of the happy news last evening." He sighed soulfully. "Surely there must be easier ways to make a living."

If there were, I had no doubt Signore Tonetti would find them. "This will only take one night, Tonetti," I said bracingly. "A few short hours, and you will be a rich man. And you aren't running any risks—you don't have to retrieve the paper."

"True enough," he agreed, brightening like the heartless creature he was. "It is you they will catch, and I'll be long gone." His smile of satisfaction grated, and I put a loverlike hand on his lavender forearm and pinched him, hard.

"It would be best," I said icily, a sweet smile on my face, "if neither of us is caught. I'm counting on you to see to that. When are we going to do this?"

He pulled himself together. "He leaves tomorrow afternoon. Tomorrow night I will come and fetch you, sometime around nine. You'll get rid of the little bambina, yes?"

"Yes, I'll get rid of Maggie."

"We will stop first at a shop I know of, where you will change your clothes. Something a bit more suited to an Austrian whore. We'll continue on to the barracks, I'll escort you to the general's rooms, and from then on you're on your own. A few moments' search, a simple escape, and all will be well."

"And what if someone questions my presence?" I demanded, unmoved by this rosy picture.

"Signorina del Zaglia, with the dress and face paint I will provide, and the physical attributes nature so generously endowed you with, you will have no trouble at all lulling the suspicions of an entire platoon of Tedeschi. All you have to do is bat your eyes like this"—he demonstrated, and I had to stifle a burst of laughter—"and show some of your lovely . . . er . . . chest, and the Tedeschi will forget their questions. Trust me, Madonna."

I allowed him an overlong salute to my glove, and smiled benevolently. "Tomorrow night at nine, my pigeon," he announced thrillingly. "But now I must fly."

And fly he did, leaving me watching his mincing figure depart with mixed emotions. Contempt, amusement, and a very real fear warred within me for control. God help me if I failed tomorrow night! Tonetti certainly wouldn't.

As I turned I came face to face with that bastion of England, Florian's Café. I hardly even felt surprise as I recognized one dark gold head alone at a distant table, one pair of silver-blue eyes watching me with mingled curiosity and irritation before he buried himself once more in his paper.

I hesitated for only a moment. Tomorrow I could very well die—today I intended to seize every last moment of life that I could. With a graceful self-assurance I was far from feeling, I seated myself opposite Evan Fitzpatrick.

He lowered the newspaper slowly, those eyes meeting mine with an unreadable expression in their smoky depths. Before he could open his mouth to order me away, however, an eager waiter appeared at the table with the customary, "Behold me!"

Evan hesitated, but only for a moment. "Two coffees," he said tersely, and then flashed the smile that he seemed to reserve for everyone but me. The waiter responded, as he couldn't help but do, and ran off to do his bidding. And then the silver-blue eyes swung back to me, and of course the smile vanished.

"Your admirer desert you?" he questioned coldly. "He should have seen you home. I would have thought you learned your lesson yesterday. Venice is a dangerous place for an unescorted lady. I hadn't thought to see you again."

The thought didn't seem to faze him in the least. "Whereas I rather thought I would see you," I replied in a low voice. "So I had no need of another escort." I smiled brilliantly across the table. "Don't glower at me like that—it doesn't become you. You might as well accept your fate."

A look of reluctant amusement warmed the chilly depths of his eyes. "Now I'm sure you're about to tell me what that fate is, aren't you, my dove?"

I smiled serenely. "Indeed. Though you know it as well as I do."

The coffee arrived and Evan stirred it absently, his eyes never leaving my face. For a moment he seemed lost in thought, and I leaned back and sipped the strong, bitter brew, happy just to be sitting in the sunshine in that glorious square, across from the man I knew I would love.

Finally he seemed to come to a decision, and his face was infinitely soft and beguiling as he spoke. So beguiling, in fact, that he only stiffened my resolve.

"My dear Lucy, you are being absurd. You've only just met me, we've never even been formally introduced, and yet you have cast maidenly decorum to the winds in a misguided fascination for me. I can't believe England is so lacking in young men that you would be desperate enough to have fancied a passion for an aging adventurer like me. A young lady with your very considerable physical charms could hardly have been lacking in admirers. Unless England has changed a great deal in the last two years."

"Two years?" I echoed, fastening on this last piece of information. "But what about your son? Haven't you seen him in that long?"

His face darkened, and I knew that once more I had overstepped the bounds of propriety. "My son is in the very capable hands of my brother Simon and his wife. They both adore him, and no doubt Jamie is far better off without me around."

The bitter expression was back around his mouth, and I wanted to kiss it away.

"Do you think he feels that way?" I asked in a low voice, wondering whether he would throw his coffee cup at me. I wouldn't have blamed him.

"No, Miss del Zaglia, he doesn't feel that way. But he will, sooner or later. He'll have no choice."

"And are you better off without him around?"

A bitter laugh escaped him. "No, I'm not. But I have enough sense to realize what is best for Jamie. I only wish you had the sense to keep your lovely little nose out of other people's business."

I met his gaze calmly, unabashed. "I am tactless," I admitted, "and indiscreet. You will have to work on curing me of it."

Another long silence. "Lucy," he said gently, "you know nothing about me."

I took another sip from my coffee, hoping it would take long, blissful hours to finish the tiny cup. "I know a great deal just from looking at you," I replied evenly.

"Such as?" he mocked. "You can tell that I'm scarred, bitter, and nasty to young girls. You are only lucky that I haven't given way to my baser instincts and become even nastier, and in more devastating ways."

I ignored him. "I can tell a great many things about you. You're obviously idealistic, or you wouldn't be so very cynical all the time. People are only cynical when their ideals have been betrayed." I leaned back in my chair, prepared to enjoy this, putting my fingertips together in a meditative fashion. "I would say, and this is sheer conjecture, mind you, that you would be the type to love the country rather than the city, fishing rather than hunting, old, smelly spaniels rather than beagles or bloodhounds."

I had caught his attention for sure this time. "You are surprisingly accurate," he said softly. "Continue."

"Well"—I thought for a moment, warming to my subject—"you would prefer Venice to Paris, Scotland to England, old ballads and sea chanteys to classical arias. You must have a lovely bass voice," I added absently.

"Not too bad," he admitted. "Go on."

"You prefer riding to driving even the most elegant curricle. You don't want to be tied to anyone or anything. You love the sea and the mountains, you read a lot. You're capable of killing, if necessary. And I think you're still capable of loving."

His eyes narrowed. "Very astute. And who have you been talking with?"

"No one. I just know you."

"You are astonishingly correct on every suit,

but you forgot I like cats, too. You also neglected to mention my taste in women." There was a challenge there, and reluctantly I drained the last of my coffee.

I let my eyes wander over the long, lean length of him, the overlong dark blond hair, the tanned, scarred face with those fathomless blue eyes surrounded by tiny little lines, the broad shoulders, the long, slender hands that could snuff out a life so easily, that could bring me to life just as carelessly. I smiled, a small, sad, weary smile. "You probably have the execrable taste to prefer tiny, fragile, little blonde ladies."

One of those hands reached across the table and captured mine and held it lightly, so that it was hard to remember the steely strength in those long, thin fingers. "And that's where you're wrong," he said gently, throwing caution to the winds. "I much prefer tall, statuesque ladies with hair like the night, eyes like honey, warm and sweet, and soft, rounded bodies with just the right curves." He brought my hand to his mouth for a lingering moment, and I felt absurdly like crying. "But I also have enough sense never to seduce infatuated virgins, either highborn or otherwise. This will be the last time I warn you, Lucy. Go away. Go as far away and as fast as you can. The next time I might not let you leave." And he dropped my

The Demon Count's Daughter

hand, stood up, and strode swiftly away from me through the rapidly increasing crowd, only the slightest trace of a limp reminding me of his wound. And if he had turned back he would have seen a smile of wicked triumph light my face.

CHAPTER TWELVE

That evening and the next day passed far too swiftly, and yet the hours seemed to drag at a snail's pace. I had always thought I was so very brave, but the thought of dressing in some revealing evening dress and brazening my way into a gentleman's bedroom filled me with icy foreboding. That small, baser part of me wanted desperately to run back to Evan Fitzpatrick's small apartment by La Fenice, to fling myself against his broad chest and pour out the insane thing I was planning to do. He would never let me; he would go in my stead.

And be caught, and hanged, I thought wearily, knowing that I had no choice. As I paced around the bedroom my anxious mind thought irritably, Where the hell was Uncle Mark when I really needed him? Anyone with a small portion of brain would guess what I had planned and stop me. But not dimwitted, gullible Uncle Mark. He believed every word his devious goddaughter told him and was no doubt enjoying himself royally with the blue-haired widow.

Well, there was no hope for it. I would be waiting to meet Tonetti tonight, and if I failed to survive, well, nobler people than I had perished in the cause of a free Venice.

And if I did survive, and succeed, I wouldn't return to Edentide. I would have Tonetti take me straight to Evan's apartment, where I would pour out the whole reckless tale to him and receive whatever comfort I could manage to elicit from his cold, restricted soul. Remembering his last words to me, I had no doubt his response would be sufficient.

"Is something wrong with you, Miss Luciana?" Maggie asked the next evening when I had stalked the salon floor for the better part of an hour, each time ending up by the little balcony. "You haven't eaten a thing all day, you're nervous as a cat, and I know for sure you barely slept last night. I could hear you tossing and turning and muttering."

I managed a convincing laugh. "Something wrong, Maggie?" I echoed innocently. "Nothing's wrong. I suppose I'm just homesick. I don't think this Tonetti will ever contact me."

Maggie's eyes narrowed, and I wondered for a moment whether she was really fooled. "I was thinking of asking Mr. Ferland to stop by this evening after dinner and see if he's heard anything. We can't stay here forever, you know, miss. Your parents should be returning before long, and I'd hate to have to arrive after they did."

"No!" I protested wildly, and then managed to smile weakly. "Don't bother Uncle Mark. I'm sure he'll come by as soon as he hears anything. Perhaps you're right though. I *am* exhausted. I couldn't sleep a wink last night. I think I'll go to bed early tonight and try to make up for it." I yawned widely, my eyes taking in the ornate clock hands. A quarter to nine.

"It's early yet!" Maggie protested. "You'll just lie in bed and toss and turn."

"No, I won't," I yawned again. On impulse I moved across the room and gave her a brief, bone-cracking hug. "I'll sleep like the dead." A shiver passed over me at my unfortunate choice of words. "I love you, Maggie."

"Well, I love you too," she replied, surprised. "Are you sure you're all right?"

"Positive! Good night." And I made my escape before she could ask another importunate question.

Tonetti was waiting for me by the corner of the deserted side canal. I could smell his lilac scent long before I saw him, and once more he was in his gondolier's garb. He helped me down into the rocking boat, his damp hands betraying his nervousness, and for once I was spared his flowery compliments. The stop at the small, dirty-smelling tailor's shop was far too short, just long enough for me to don an ornate, somewhat tattered gold satin dress still reeking of cheap scent from its last wearer, the top of the dress practically nonexistent. In vain I tugged at the lace bertha in an attempt to restore some measure of modesty to my toilette. It was hopeless. It was also, I had to admit, outrageously flattering.

Tonetti himself painted my face, his eyes straying toward my décolletage at every other stroke. "Signorina," he breathed, when he had finished and was able to master his emotions, "if you should ever be in need of money, I know of any number of gentlemen . . ." he swallowed. "God but you are lovely," he muttered in Italian. "Such amazing . . ." the last word I didn't understand, but his meaning was inescapable. I considered slapping him, but thought better of it. I needed all the help I could get tonight, so I merely inclined my head graciously, the thick, black locks in their slatternly arrangement tumbling over my shoulders.

It was all deceptively simple. When we arrived at one of the side entrances of the imposing building that was housing the upper classes of the

Austrian army, there was no one guarding the portal. Tonetti gestured proudly to his narrow chest. "A few bribes, Signorina, are worth the money." The long, cavernous hallway was practically deserted, and as we walked silently down the marble passageway, I could hear my heart pounding. It must be after ten, I reasoned, and then the pounding ceased. A very tall, very broad, slightly drunken Austrian officer was making his way toward us, a gleam in his slightly glazed eye. I kept my gaze demurely lowered, trying not to panic as I heard Tonetti's desperate intake of breath.

"And where is this lovely creature going, eh?" he demanded when we came abreast of him. "She must be new around here. What is your price, villain?" This was all delivered in a very jovial tone of voice, and thankfully Tonetti was able to answer him in the same manner, albeit with just the right amount of subservience due the conquering army.

"She is for the General Eisenhopf, Captain." He spread his hands in a gesture of apology. "What can I say? When he has tired of her I will be sure to keep you in mind."

I could feel the man's hot eyes raking over me, my tumbled black hair, absurd height, and practically exposed breasts. He sighed gustily. "I doubt he'll tire of her for a long, long while. More's the pity." He stumbled on, and Tonetti and I breathed a sigh of relief, our eyes meeting in momentary accord.

We met only one more soldier, and the same tactics worked beautifully. Tonetti, in fact, was getting quite cocky, and I had to restrain him from bargaining for my future price. "For the general," he contented himself with muttering importantly. And then at last we were in the corridor outside his rooms, the long, narrow, tomblike passageway dark and deserted.

"You're sure he's out of town?" I demanded in a whisper. "There's no chance he could suddenly return?"

"Signorina, trust me! He is gone, not to return till the day after tomorrow. No one else lives on this floor, and my brother-in-law is right now with my wife drinking Bardolino and getting very sleepy. All you have to do is search his rooms and then meet me down by the entranceway."

"You aren't going to wait for me?" I shrieked in a very loud whisper.

Tonetti looked suitably disheartened. "Much as I would like to, Madonna, I dare not. Someone must keep the gondola ready for our escape. If anyone questions you, reply as I have, that you are for General Eisenhopf. As you leave, simply say you grew tired of waiting."

"But what will the stupid paper look like?" I demanded desperately.

"According to my brother-in-law, it's on blue parchment with the seal of Franz Josef on it. And he hinted it might be somewhere near the bed. That is what made me think of using a woman for this."

"I'm sure that's not all that made you think of it, you coward," I muttered, panic making me rude. "Go away, then. I only hope to God I meet you when this is over."

He struck a pose. "I will await you though my life depends on it."

"You'd better," I grumbled, opening the door and slipping inside the darkened room.

I leaned against the door for a moment, long enough to still the clamoring of my pounding heart. Now that the time had actually come, I couldn't afford to waste a second in needless panic. A few moments later I had a small lamp lit, and I surveyed the room in dismay.

There were a thousand places a paper could be hidden. The desk was littered with thick piles of official documents. More covered the chairs and tables, even the bedside stand had its share of reports and documents and such.

A long and desperate hour later I seemed to be no closer to finding it, and the panic began creeping back into my thoughts. All sorts of interesting information resided in General Eisenhopf's room, but not the piece I wanted.

I looked with distaste at the big, sagging featherbed, loaded with quilts and blankets. The first search had turned up nothing more than a tiny, pearl-handled pistol. On impulse I slid my hands under the heavy mattress and found the crackle of paper.

With shaking hands I drew it out into the fitful light. It was there in my hands, a thin scrap of official parchment that had caused me to risk my life, that could mean the difference between freedom and captivity for the ancient city of Venice. I stared at it in dumfounded bemusement for too long a moment and then tucked it down inside my bodice, letting it rest against my skin.

"Ah, and what is this?" A voice boomed out, and to my horror I came face to face with a burly, much-decorated, elderly Austrian soldier standing in the bedroom door. And I knew without a doubt that General Eisenhopf had returned.

CHAPTER THIRTEEN

He moved closer into the light, closing the heavy door behind him. "And where did you come from, my little pigeon?" he cooed in German.

I kept my face a perfect blank, aided by the overwhelming terror I felt. "I . . . I am a present for the General Eisenhopf," I stammered idiotically in deliberately terrible German.

The leer on the weathered old face broadened, and he moved so close I could see the tiny, burst blood vessels in his large red nose. "But how delightful, Fräulein. How happy I am that I had to return early. And what a present, mein Gott! For the man who has everything, hein?" One meaty fist reached out and grabbed my breast, pinching hard. In another moment he had pulled my terrified, unresisting body against his large stomach, and greedy hands were pawing over my bodice, freeing my breasts from their meager confines. A wave of revulsion swept over me, causing me to shudder helplessly.

"Ah, you like that, liebchen?" the old lecher

smiled, cheerfully misunderstanding my shiver. "And there will be a lot more for you, little one. I will . . ." I shut my eyes against the wave of nausea his filthy words were eliciting from me. I was helpless in his grasp, praying desperately for some form of deliverance. And then, knowing no deliverance would come, I trampled on his instep, eliciting a roar of pain. I then brought my knee up in his groin, my elbow in his throat, and ran, leaving the poor old man howling in pain and rage.

Down the deserted halls I ran, certain that pursuit was just barely behind me. But luck was with me, and I met no one. I was able to restore a small amount of modesty to my mauled attire, and at the end of the final corridor I saw the canal glistening in the moonlight, Tonetti pacing nervously back and forth.

"Did you find the general, little one?" A voice questioned close behind me, and I whirled to meet the gaze of the drunken young soldier.

I laughed convincingly. "I grew tired of waiting," I replied in my atrocious German. "He will have to wait for another night."

"But then you are free to spend the evening with me!" he said joyfully, and I shook my head with a great show of reluctance.

"Unfortunately not. I was promised to the general first. If he finds anyone has had me before him, I would hate to think of the consequences." Deliberately I bent over a bit, letting him ogle my cleavage. "For you as well as me."

"True enough," he agreed sadly, his eyes feasting on my frontage. "But be sure you look me up when he's finished, eh?"

"Of course," I soothed. He turned his back, and I ran the last few steps to the dubious haven of Tonetti's gondola.

"I have it!" I crowed in a triumphant whisper, fumbling with the front of my dress as I tried to dislodge the tricky paper. Finally catching hold of it, I thrust it proudly into his reluctant hands. "We've got to get out of here, fast! The general caught me. Everyone will be looking for us in a few moments. We'd better . . ."

"There she is!" A shout echoed through the building, and, looking up, I saw a pair of cold, evil eyes staring down at me from the overhanging balcony. Holger von Wolfram, accompanied by the two Venetian villains of the Doges' Palace. He pointed a beefy arm at me. "Get her!" he ordered roughly. "Kill her if you must, but get her."

Without waiting for Tonetti I took off into the night, my tattered satin dress waving behind me, my hair down around my bare shoulders, panic making my heart close to bursting. But one overlarge woman is a lot quieter than a platoon of Austrian soldiers. Each time I heard them gaining on me I would duck into one of the numerous alleyways and wait until the streets were silent once more. I knew I had a great deal more to fear from the two Italian henchmen, and even when the streets seemed deserted I moved warily, edging inexorably toward my goal. The apartment by the La Fenice.

And then suddenly the theater loomed in front of me, and I broke into a run. Up Evan's stairs like a terrified rabbit, banging on his door and calling his name. I looked back over my shoulder and saw the doorway darken, and I increased my pounding, desperation tearing at my vitals. What if he were out? Would I be murdered in this small, already blood-stained hallway?

And then the door opened, and I fell into the room, sobbing with relief and fright, and felt my trembling body enfolded into a strong, comforting embrace.

It took me a few moments to regain my composure. When at last I was able to stop the shuddering, reluctantly I moved away and looked up into Evan's quizzical, concerned eyes. "Thank God you were here," I said simply.

The concern vanished, to be replaced by the

blazing anger I saw so often in those silver-blue eyes. "What the hell," he began coldly, "are you doing out alone at this hour of the night? Why are you dressed like a strumpet? And what are you doing here? I thought you were safely asleep at Edentide."

"I was followed . . ." I began lamely.

"I don't doubt you were followed," he cut in. "Half the men in Venice were probably trailing you through the streets, what with you dressed like that! Have you no sense at all?"

"It wasn't like that!" I defended myself. "I . . . I . . ." I was about to pour out the terror of my night's adventures, the long, involved tale of my crazy mission to Venice, when I noticed for the first time my surroundings. Evan was dressed, or partially dressed, in a pair of soft gray pants and a hastily donned shirt unbuttoned to show the broad, tanned expanse of his chest. I noticed with distracted lust that it was covered with fine, golden hair. Beyond him was a candlelit table, the remains of a supper for two littered across the snowy cloth. A woman's evening cloak lay across the sofa, and from beyond the bedroom door I could hear furtive movements.

Evan must have heard them too. "Excuse me a moment," he said roughly, and moved with a barely perceptible limp toward the bedroom door.

"Stay there!" he ordered over his shoulder, shutting the door behind his broad back.

The murmur of voices came to me, his deep and cool, and a light, laughing German voice. I thought back to the blonde at the embassy in dismay and began backing toward the door. This last was more than I could stand—the triumph of retrieving the paper was like ashes in my mouth.

In my confusion I bumped into the desk, knocking a sheaf of papers onto the floor. Picking them up, my eye caught only a line or two. Hastily I shoved them back on the desk and turned to run from the place, the contents branded into my mind. I knew from my sojourn in the general's rooms that they were official Austrian papers, and I knew without a doubt I was in the company of a spy. But a spy for whom?

"Where are you going?" The door shut behind him, and in the dim light I couldn't make out his face.

"I . . . I . . ." I stammered witlessly, "I'm sorry to interrupt you. It was stupid of me. I thought . . ."

"You thought what?"

"I don't know," I floundered, smiling up at him, the tears brilliant in my eyes. "I am very gauche, I'm afraid. I didn't think." My hand reached the brass doorknob and I turned it quickly.

"Wait a moment," he ordered, and I thought I could detect a softening in his voice. "Let me get my coat and I'll see you home."

"No!" I cried in a strangled voice. The softening could only be brought on by pity, and pity was the last thing I wanted from Evan Fitzpatrick. "I'll be perfectly all right, I assure you." I kept the silly smile firmly affixed to my painted face as I felt the tears trickle down my cheeks. "I don't . . ." Words failed me, and on a choked sob I ran from the apartment into the dangerous streets of Venice, running once more from Evan Fitzpatrick.

As my thin leather slippers sped across the cobblestones, I thought I could hear a voice calling my name, loud, in almost desperation. A voice that sounded like Evan, but I couldn't be sure. Heedlessly I dodged into an alleyway, then into another, till I came slap up against a totally unfamiliar canal. I heard a soft footstep behind me, and as I whirled around I felt something hard come down behind my ear, and everything went black.

CHAPTER FOURTEEN

As consciousness slowly returned I became aware of a great many unpleasant things. An aching head was the first of my worries, followed by a cramped, stiff body, the stifling folds of a fish-scented tarpaulin preventing any fresh air from reaching me, and the steady rhythm of oars behind me. It didn't take the even rocking of the gondola to tell me I was in a boat; my riotous stomach, usually so sanguine about sea travel, was making it perfectly clear. Grimly I swallowed the bile that threatened to rise in my throat and kept my cramped, stiff limbs perfectly still.

Without moving more than a few pertinent muscles I could tell that I had been neither bound nor gagged. Apparently my captors considered the blow to my head enough to keep me immobile for hours. Indeed, it could have been hours since they clobbered me; I had no way of knowing.

"Durano is up ahead," one villain muttered in non-Venetian Italian. "Is she still out?"

A not-too-gentle foot prodded my posterior.

"Still dreaming like a babe," another answered, chuckling evilly. "The two of us might have a bit of trouble carrying a bambina like that, eh?" And I knew with mingled horror and relief that it was the two Italian brigands from the Doges' Palace who'd finally caught up with me, and with a chill I remembered Holger's orders to them. "Kill her if you must, but get her." I should have stayed in Evan's apartment, no matter how *de trop* I was.

By amazing luck Evan had been able to rescue me before, but given the circumstances there was no way I could count on his help again. No doubt at this moment he was lost in the arms of his Austrian whore, far too involved in whatever deep game he was playing to spare a thought for me, on a boat ride to death.

I lay very, very still, tensing my muscles, and then in a sudden leap was over the side of the small boat, the fishy tarp following me like a cape. And then the water hit like a shock of ice, and I dove beneath the surface with more speed than care.

I was well paid for it. The water was only about four feet deep, and I hit my nose on an outcropping of rock. I surfaced briefly and found my shoulders caught in a punishing grip.

"Not so sleepy, eh?" the great hulking creature demanded with the travesty of a smile. "The signorina is far too eager to walk upon the shore, Gianni. Shall we drag her behind the boat?"

"Pull her in, Ricci," the other replied in a bored tone of voice. "After we get to the house you can amuse yourself with her."

As I was unceremoniously pulled into the gondola I kept my limbs a dead weight, hoping against hope to tip the rocking craft. But Gianni, despite his non-Venetian accent, knew his way around a gondola, and I was dumped onto the seat with a casual cuff to the side of my head. I lay there in a mild stupor for another twenty minutes until the stars began to clear from in front of my eyes, listening with sick dread as they made their plans for my soon-to-be-departed virginity. I think I would have preferred that they murder me.

By the time we reached the shore a heavy, blinding fog had settled in, obscuring the land, the faces of my captors, and even a hand in front of my eyes. With stumbling, awkward feet I followed the first man, aided by a rough push every now and then from his trailing companion that would send me sprawling on the rough dirt.

I needed all my senses to keep me going. The island, or so I assumed it to be, appeared uninhabited; no lights or sound penetrated the thick, thick fog that sank through my heavy, wet, clinging clothes and into the marrow of my bones.

"You want her first, Ricci?" the first man inquired courteously, and I could sense him turning in front of me. "It's all right with me if you do; I can always watch. Von Wolfram has said he no longer cares what we do with her."

"No, you go first," his companion replied with equal generosity. "Just leave something for me, eh?" His laugh chilled me more than the cold, dank fog. "Though there looks like more than enough for both of us in this one, my friend." He put one meaty paw in my back and once more I tripped.

It was miraculous that I was able to keep my balance, but my sudden equilibrium displeased Ricci, who was longing for the chance to kick my fallen body.

"Stupid slut," he muttered, crashing his heavy hand across my face. I stood there, still upright but swaying ever so slightly. I saw his hand upraised and numbly felt it connect with the other side of my face. I fell then, and lay on the rough dirt, every part of my body aching, knowing a good, hard kick was coming at any moment. I lay there immobile, determined not to cringe.

The kick never came. A sudden scuffle sounded behind me, a muffled oath, and the sound of a fist hitting flesh.

"Ricci?" Gianni spoke from up ahead, a worried note to his guttural voice. "Are you all right?"

Another thud, and then silence. Slowly, painfully, I struggled to a sitting position, my eyes trying to focus through the thick, gray fog. A seemingly huge, dark figure loomed ahead of me, with a horrendous humped back, hideously like something out of Victor Hugo. I stifled a small scream of terror as it came closer and then nearly fainted with astonishment and relief as I recognized it.

Evan had the body of the first bandit across his shoulders, giving him a nightmare quality in silhouette. "Stay there," he muttered tersely, moving around me with his burden. A few moments later he was back, picking up the second man and hauling him away with the same careless strength. And then finally there he was, his big, strong hands lifting me to my feet, his face through the mist no longer cold and angry but filled with a warm, loving concern.

I didn't even stop to question his miraculous appearance. I was still so stunned I merely accepted him as my *deus ex machina*. "Did you kill them?" I questioned, and was startled to hear my voice come out in a tiny croak.

He shook his head, the damp strands loose around his scarred face. "I dumped them in their gondola and pushed them out to sea. The tide should carry them to the mainland in a day or two."

"Won't they come back here?" The feel of his hands beneath my elbows was warm and comforting, and I barely stifled a protest as he withdrew them.

"I neglected to leave them with an oar. By the time they reach land and get back here, you'll be long gone. Out of Venice and halfway back to England."

It would be useless to question his arrogant assumption, so I said nothing. "How in the world did you get here?" My curiosity was reviving.

"By boat, of course. I've been only a short way behind you since you ran off into the night like a hysterical child. When the fog settled I was afraid I'd lost you for certain, but they'd just reached Durano. If they'd planned to go on I would have given up." His voice was flat and emotionless, but his eyes burned in the pale, fog-shrouded face, and deep within me I knew he would have followed us halfway across the Adriatic before he let them get away with me. Despite my chilled, wet garments I felt suddenly warm.

"Can you take me back?"

"Not tonight. I was barely able to navigate following those two brigands. In this dense fog we wouldn't stand a chance . . . we'd reach the mainland just in time to welcome your energetic enemies." He turned around. "No, we'll have to find some sort of shelter and wait till the fog lifts. It should be clear by mid-morning, at the latest."

I viewed this last piece of news with surprising equanimity. "Does anyone live on this island? Someone who could take us in till morning?"

He shook his head, peering through the fog with narrowed eyes. "Entirely uninhabited. Why do you think they brought you here?"

"I have no idea, other than the obvious one," I lied. I could no longer dare to trust him, much as I longed to. Apparently he wasn't much interested in my conjectures, for he moved off into the night, and I let out a small shriek that sent him rushing back to my side.

"What's wrong?" he demanded irritably.

"I would greatly appreciate it," I said in a stiff voice, "if you would control your distaste for me long enough to give me your arm while we wander around in the dark. I happen to be cold and wet and frightened. If it's too much for you, of course, please don't bother." My voice was frigid with rage and a barely controlled panic.

To my surprise a grin lit his face, and I felt my heart do a casual little leap within me. "My pleasure, madame." He bowed, offering his arm like a courtier. "I will try to smother the normal disgust and repulsion I feel toward you for the time being, though it is very, very difficult."

Placing my hand on his forearm I could feel the steely strength of his muscles through the fine linen shirt. "Please do," I replied with distant courtesy. "And I will do my best not to compromise one of your tender sensibilities."

"You are too kind," he murmured, starting off at a slower pace through the impenetrable fog.

It was a rough journey. My slippers were in tatters, the satin dress completely destroyed by its sojourn in the sea. My head ached, my cheek throbbed, and it seemed to me I was colder than I had ever been in my life. Through it all the only comfort I had was the feel of Evan's arm beneath my hand, the certain knowledge that he would lead me to safety.

Instead he led me to a small, doorless, practically roofless cottage, sitting all alone in the midst of a damp and nasty-smelling swamp. His eyesight in the dark was far better than mine, and he steered my suddenly nerveless body to a narrow pallet on the floor. I collapsed in exhaustion and lay there, listening dazedly as he struggled with some slightly damp lucifers. A moment later the meager light from a candle stub illuminated the hovel, and hovel it certainly was. The floor was dirt, the giant fireplace filled with wet, smelly ashes, and not a trace of food in the house. For the first time I realized how incredibly hungry I was, and a small groan escaped me.

"Don't you like it?" Evan demanded, and there was a curiously light note in his voice. One might almost have thought he was enjoying the whole miserable situation.

I summoned up my last ounce of courage. "Well, it's not quite as cozy as Edentide, but I suppose, given the circumstances, it will do." I watched in distrust as Evan disappeared into the next room.

"There's a bed in there," he said calmly, coming back into the room. "I suggest you get out of that absurd rag and try to get some sleep. I wouldn't dare attempt to get us out of here before daylight, even if the fog happens to lift sooner." He peered out the open door into the night. "I'll sleep here and keep watch."

For some reason I felt as if I'd been slapped in the face. "Keep watch for what?" I questioned stiffly.

He smiled an enigmatic smile. "There's always the chance your two admirers' paymaster might arrive. Durano is a perfect meeting place for people not wishing to be seen. Go on in and get some sleep. Tomorrow you can tell me what the hell you've been doing, wandering around Venice at all hours of the night dressed like that." His voice was like that of an indulgent parent, and I found myself with the curious urge to scream.

"Could we possibly have a fire?" I requested in a very small voice, trying to control my shivers.

"I'm afraid not." He sounded repulsively cheerful. "That would lead anyone who happened to be near the island straight to us. Once you get out of those wet clothes you'll feel warmer. Run along now."

I bit back the retort that rose to my lips as I struggled to my feet, the wet, ruined satin dress dragging around my ankles. If Evan Fitzpatrick felt safer treating me like an infant, that was his problem and not my own.

The inner room was pitch black, and I bumped into the bed, banging my knees painfully. I climbed into the sagging, creaking, no doubt flea-ridden mattress, and sat there, wet and miserable and cold and hungry. And alone. I sincerely doubted if I had ever been so unhappy in my entire life, and as my chilled, wet fingers fumbled with the myriad of tiny buttons, warm tears began sliding down my face. The buttons refused to yield to my clumsy fingers; the wet satin was too strong to rip, and I was about to throw myself down and cry my heart out when I felt, rather than heard, Evan behind me.

"You are a helpless one, aren't you?" he said softly, his voice and hands curiously gentle as he undid the buttons. It took him a long time, hampered as he was with my long curtain of sea-damp hair, the slippery satin, and the heavy, comforting blackness of the room. When he finished he moved away abruptly, before I had a chance to turn around, and his voice came from the doorway.

"Leave your dress at the foot of the bed and I'll hang it up later. There's a blanket beside your head ... that should help. Good night." There was a great deal of finality in his voice, a finality I could scarcely argue with.

"Good night," I said in muffled misery, dumping my sodden dress on the dirt floor and tossing my cotton petticoats beside it. Some last vestige of modesty made me keep my chemise and pantalets on. He had seen me in them already, the time of my other abortive swim, and it hadn't seemed to arouse him then either. Sighing, I pulled the thin, thankfully clean-smelling blanket around my shivering body and tried to go to sleep.

CHAPTER FIFTEEN

It was later, much later, when I awoke. My thin, cotton underclothing was sticking to my body like sheets of ice, my skin was covered with goose bumps, and my teeth chattered like castanets. I clamped hard on my jaw, biting my tongue in the process, and had to cope with the pain along with the dreadful, dreadful cold. I couldn't will my body to be still . . . the shivers that racked it made the bed squeak loudly in the silent cottage. I was trembling so hard I thought my bones would rattle loose in their sockets, and vainly I tried to find some warmth in the thin blanket I was huddled under. But there seemed to be no warmth there.

Suddenly I could stand it no longer. As surreptitiously as I could I crept from the bed, the thin blanket wrapped around my frigid body. The outer room was still pitch black, and silently I tiptoed past the pallet where I knew Evan would be sleeping, terrified that I should wake him. As I stepped outside I noticed with relief that the fog had lifted and a strong, clear moonlight was streaming through the clouds. The air was only slightly warmer, and even more damp, and I did the only thing possible. I dropped the blanket on the ground, and, barefoot, clad only in thin, damp, lace underclothing, I took off at a dead run across the now visible hill in front of the tiny house.

Ten minutes later I was back, panting, sweating, and gloriously warm and alive. The moonlight was very bright, and as I reached for my blanket I straightened up and looked straight into Evan's eyes.

"You must," he said slowly, "be entirely crazy."

The moonlight silvered his dark blond hair, gilded the planes of his face, and practically obscured the long, fascinating scar. With his linen shirt open to the waist I could see other, more recent scars on his broad, strong chest, and I wondered what kind of life he lived that would leave its mark so starkly on his lovely body.

"Not entirely," I replied huskily. "I was very cold." A random shiver passed over my body, and belatedly I realized how very immodest my attire was, illuminated there in the moonlight. Not that that cold-hearted, goddamned man cared.

"You're going to be a lot colder in a few moments. A good case of pneumonia should keep you out of trouble for the next few months." His eyes were narrowed and unreadable, entirely unmoved by my overripe body in the thin scraps of cloth. Mentally I shrugged.

Another shiver ran over me, and then another. "I suppose you're right," I said through chattering teeth, suddenly weak hands fumbling with the thin blanket that would provide me with scarcely any protection.

He moved quickly then, so quickly I scarcely saw him. In another moment the blanket was securely around me, and I was lifted in his arms as effortlessly as if I were one of those fragile blondes I was so envious of. For a moment I was blissfully, delightfully warm, and then he dumped me unceremoniously on the pallet.

As he towered over me I felt very small, very fragile, and very weak. It was a delicious feeling for a change.

He squatted down beside me, every line in his lean face visible in the soft moonlight streaming through the open door, and one gentle hand reached out and touched my cheek. I winced, and his mouth tightened grimly.

"Perhaps I should have killed them," he said in a low voice, his fingers gentle on my bruised flesh. "Not that you don't deserve to be beaten."

Somewhere I found my voice. "I wish you wouldn't be so nasty. You really like me, you know you do. You wouldn't be following me around, pulling me out of scrapes, if you didn't."

He hesitated, about to say something, and then obviously thought better of it. "Perhaps I do," he conceded, "but I can't see much future in a friendship between us."

I swallowed. "I wasn't asking for friendship."

The beginnings of a small smile appeared at the corners of his well-shaped mouth, and his hand kept stroking my face. "And what were you asking for, Lucy?"

There was no way I could answer that, no way at all. I looked up at him mutely, but he wasn't the sort to let me weasel out of a situation.

"You don't really know, do you?" He was asking himself more than me. "I don't know if I've ever met such innocence before." Carelessly he pinched my other cheek and started to rise. "Go to sleep, my child, and dream of pirates."

I caught at his hand before he could move away. "Would you stay with me?" I asked, and my voice came out in a whispered croak.

His face was unreadable. "What did you say?"

"I said, Would you stay with me?" I repeated in a slightly louder voice that quavered only slightly. "I'm cold and frightened and I don't want to be alone."

He stared at me for a long moment. "You're not

making this easy, Lucy. Do you know what you're asking?"

Panic set in. "I . . . I thought it might be nice if we . . . if we just slept together. It would be comforting." I floundered helplessly before the amusement and something else in his silver-blue eyes. "I mean, without . . ."

"I know you mean without . . ." he mocked me gently. "Unfortunately for you, life doesn't work out that way."

"What do you mean?" I whispered.

"I warned you that you would push me too far, and there would be no turning back, Lucy." One hand went gently behind my neck, under my damp, heavy hair, and I felt myself being lifted gently to him. His lips met mine in a kiss that brooked no refusals, no hesitation, no subterfuge. And without thinking I answered it, giving him all of myself with my mouth.

His lips traveled along my neck, leaving a trail of burning kisses on my damp skin. One strong hand cupped my full breast, and involuntarily I stiffened.

He pulled away swiftly, as if burned, and I wanted to cry out in disappointment. "Are you going to fight me?" he asked softly, his voice husky with desire.

I shook my head slowly. "No, I won't fight you."

I put my hands behind his neck, twining my fingers through the dark blond curls, and pressed my lips against the thin, angry line of his scar. "But Evan," I whispered shyly in his ear, "be careful of me. I'm not very brave."

He looked down at me, those strong, lean hands framing my face as he sought to read everything in my eyes. "My angel," he said, and this time the endearment was not mocking, "I will be very, very careful." And pulling me into his arms, he lay down on the pallet beside me, holding me gently, comfortably, until my trembling stopped, and I was no longer cold.

With deft, careful hands he removed the poor sodden scraps of my clothing before I was even aware of it. Turning in his arms I could feel his strong, rough-textured hands on my skin, my thighs, my hips, my breasts, stroking, reassuring, exciting me in ways I had never even dared dream of. My head was pressed against his shoulder, my eyes tightly shut as he continued to caress me, and if the core of fear within me had yet to be dissolved, why then I had perfect faith that no one but Evan would be able to do it.

He smelled like salt water and leather and sweat—an enticingly masculine odor that made me snuggle deeper against him. One brave, tentative hand crept out and touched his broad chest, and I heard an approving murmur from deep within his throat as his clever, clever hands kneaded away my terror. As they reached between my thighs I stiffened once more in fright, but this time he refused to back off. With gentle, inexorable strength he forced them apart, stroking gently, murmuring soft, comforting words until his hand found me, and I stiffened with something other than fear as he began a new sort of caress, one that made my hips arch in pleasure, and my hands gripped Evan's shoulders tightly as I tried to stifle the gasp of joy that escaped my lips.

Pulling my head away from the comforting haven of his shoulders, I looked up and met his shadowy eyes. I kissed his mouth, opening mine beneath his probing tongue, and my body shivered with delight. Tentatively I ran my hands along the smooth, lean sides of him, over his firm, flat stomach. And then his hand grasped mine and brought it lower, so that I caught and held him. A groan of pleasure sounded in the back of his throat, and I felt a small surge of triumph wash over me, that I was able to give something back to him.

"God," he muttered softly, as his mouth moved along my skin, "you are so damned beautiful."

I squirmed beneath his hands, my breath coming in short, shallow gasps, longing for something

I didn't recognize. "So are you," I said in a soft, breathless laugh, and found myself a victim once more of that fierce, gentle, demanding mouth.

And then his big, strong body covered mine, crushing any last protests I might have made. As one hand smoothed my tangled hair away from my forehead, the other parted my thighs. "This will hurt, my love, but only for a moment." And then I felt first a gentle pressure, gradually increasing till there was a sharp moment of agonizing pain. And then it was past, and my body relaxed in the aftermath of the sharp, cruel hurt.

"Is that all?" I whispered in Evan's ear, my lips touching the old scar once more.

He looked down at me and smiled, a look of inexpressible tenderness in his usually cold eyes. "No," he murmured. "The best part is left." And with that he began to move, very slowly and gently at first, gradually increasing as he could feel me respond. The heat surged through my loins, and I could feel the pressure building, building, until I thought I might explode. And then, to my amazement, I did, as I felt myself flooded with warmth, and the moonlit room swirled away into nothingness, and all I knew was Evan's lovely, strong body within me, his rough voice murmuring, "Now, now." And I heard a sharp cry of pleasure in the dimness and recognized it as my own.

After a long while, when our breathing had returned to normal, he moved off me, his arms still keeping me prisoner against his broad, strong chest. I could hear the racing of his heart, could feel my own beating a similar tattoo. "Christ," I said fervently, "I do love you." My only response was a tightening in his arms. But for the time being that was enough.

CHAPTER SIXTEEN

I was an apt pupil. By the time the moon disappeared and the sun rose on that tiny, deserted island, I had had two more lessons in the ancient art of making love. My bones ached, my lips were bruised from kisses, and I was exceedingly tender in various strategic spots. I was also blissfully, idiotically happy as I lay wide awake in Evan's arms, listening to the sound of his heavy breathing, feeling the warmth of his body against mine. Never had I felt so in harmony with the world, and foolishly I envisioned nothing but more of such happiness in the future.

There was no reason under the sun, I decided, that Evan would have followed me, fought with me, rescued me, unless he was in love with me. It was only natural for him to fight the affliction; after a wife like his first one he was bound to be nervous of the whole idea of love and marriage. I felt nothing but a smug pride that I had overcome his scruples thus far, and I envisioned a small, lovely little wedding in the near future.

Mother would adore him at first sight, and Father —well, he'd be a good match for my intimidating father. I couldn't wait till they met.

As Evan's eyes opened and looked down on me lying sleepily in his arms, I had the very good sense to keep all these plans to myself. He would have to come to terms with it all in his own time. That he would, sooner or later, I had no doubt.

"How long have you been awake?" he asked gently, kissing me softly on the forehead. "Didn't I wear you out enough last night?"

I chuckled softly. "You did indeed." I ran a curious hand along his thigh, tracing the recent knife wound with careful fingers, and felt his reaction. "I still have some energy left, however."

He smiled, and I was filled with such love I almost wept. "Do you now? Well, you'll have to take pity on my declining years for a bit. *You* wore *me* out."

"Good!" I sat up abruptly, not in the slightest bit self-conscious of my nude body in the early morning sunlight. "Are you sure we have to go back to Venice?"

"I thought you loved Venice?" he questioned lazily, watching me out of narrowed eyes.

"Oh, I do. But I like this little island even better. There is only one problem with it."

"And that is?"

"No food. And I am absolutely starving!"

He laughed. "Nights like last night do build up an appetite," he agreed with false sobriety. "If you can somehow make yourself decent in that rag of a dress, I will take you back to Venice and treat you to the biggest breakfast you've ever eaten."

Jumping out of bed, I examined the pathetic rag that Tonetti had procured for me. "I doubt if it will be Florian's in this apparel." I searched around the dirt floor for my scraps of underclothing and began dressing with slow, deliberate reluctance.

"There's a trattoria not far from Edentide where no one will stare too badly," he promised, watching me out of hooded eyes. "And you may have fried eels, polenta, squassetto, pasta, and whatever else pleases your greedy little heart."

As I watched him dress quickly with his usual pantherish grace I would have almost foregone all that lovely food for the sake of another day on this enchanted island. I opened my mouth to say as much, then thought better of it. Instinctively I knew better than to push Evan too far too fast. He needed time to come to terms with me, and that was the least I could give him.

Therefore I was deliberately cheerful during the long ride back to Venice. We found a small shawl to drape around my low-cut shoulders and give me at least the appearance of decency. There was no way the dress could look like anything other than a rag, but with my hairpins lost and my long, thick, black hair trailing down my back, I looked rather slatternly anyway. With Evan to protect me, I had no fear I would suffer any importunities.

True to his word, Evan fed me nobly in a small café only a few steps away from Edentide and surpassed me in appetite. The black-haired giantess with the ragged clothing did, however, create more than her share of confusion, but a glower from Evan's cold, angry eyes was enough to scare away the boldest admirer. Only one person failed to see the warning and came up with such an outrageous suggestion that my companion nearly strangled him on the spot. As it was, all Evan had to do was rise to his full, menacing height, which was almost a foot taller than the young macaroni, and the area around our table was quickly deserted.

As he sat back down again I chuckled, and his eyes met mine ruefully. "I don't suppose there's any chance you didn't understand him?"

"No chance at all. You should have named some colossal price for me . . . that would have scared him off faster than anything." I took another sip of the deliciously warm, strong coffee.

He reached out one strong hand and touched my face in a light, lingering gesture that was almost, but not quite, a caress. "He probably would have sold his mother to meet the price." The look in his eyes was inexpressibly tender, and I melted all over again. "Are you ready to go?"

It struck me then as very strange: that he had yet to ask me why I had been wandering out alone last night. However, I had enough sense not to initiate the conversation, so full of questions I didn't know yet whether I could answer. Draining my coffee, I rose. "I suppose so. Would you rather I go back alone? We're only a short ways away."

He shook his head, and I noticed a slight grimness around his well-shaped mouth. "With your luck you would be grabbed within two yards of the palazzo. I'll see you to your door."

Flattered as I was by this concern, a certain uneasiness began to play beneath my ribs. I had no idea what excuse I would give Maggie, if I would bother to lie to her at all. If she got one good look at Evan she would know the truth anyway. But still no word of the future had come from Evan's mouth, and patient though I was determined to be, I would have been much happier to have heard some expression of affection from his firmly shut lips.

Belatedly I remembered Tonetti. I had comfortably assumed that he had escaped safely last night with the all-important paper, but now doubts were beginning to cloud my assurance. As far as I could tell, the Austrians had been interested in me alone—a scented little fribble like Tonetti should have been counted as inconsequential. When I saw Uncle Mark I would have to pour out the details of the last few days of espionage and see if he could find out what happened.

We mounted the steps slowly, both of us reluctant. Before I had time to knock on the great oak door it was flung open, and a harassed and wild-eyed Maggie greeted me with a loud shriek.

"Miss Luciana!" she yelped, enfolding me into her exuberant embrace, dragging me into the darkened hallway. "Where the bloody hell have you been? We've been scared out of our minds!"

Carefully I detached her clinging hands as the door closed behind us, but to my amazement Evan was still there, his eyes unreadable, a cold, unsmiling expression about his scarred, handsome face.

"Who's we?" I questioned, a feeling of desperation settling in.

I heard a small crash ahead of me and knew

THE DEMON COUNT'S DAUGHTER

before I looked up that Uncle Mark had taken up residence in the ancient walls of Edentide.

I was totally unprepared, however, for the look of recognition and respect on his face. "Fitzpatrick!" he greeted Evan, moving past me with barely a glance and clasping his hand in a hearty grip. "I should have known that you'd be here. Did Bones arrange to have you watch over Luciana?"

For the first time in my life I felt as if I had been given a crushing blow to my vitals. I stood stock still, motionless, waiting for Evan to answer.

Those silver-blue eyes came nowhere near me. "If you'd bothered to check before you came racing after her you would have known that," he said in an unexpectedly kind voice. "Bones wouldn't have sent her off without arranging protection, Ferland. Much as I disapprove of this whole insane scheme, Bones still has *that* much sense."

"You must have been the man she saw at the train station, then," Uncle Mark continued. "What an idiot I've been! All I can do is thank God you've been around to keep an eye on the little minx. . . . At least this blasted Tonetti's never bothered to make contact. Damn it, it's no job for a lady! She could have been killed."

I kept my face averted, but I could feel Evan's

eyes rest on me, and I waited for him to expose me. "Just so," he said briefly. "The entire idea of sending a young, inexperienced female into a dangerous situation like this is not only absurd but doomed to failure. I've been trying to scare Lucy out of Venice ever since she arrived, but with no luck. I'm handing her over to you, now, Ferland. I'm sure I can count on you to see that she leaves by the early evening train?" There was a note of steel in his cool voice. "I don't have time to look after her anymore, and we can't afford having her get in the way. Besides, I'm sure Bones would like her back in one piece."

I felt my body flinch slightly as if from a blow, and I caught Maggie's sympathetic glance from out of the corner of my eye.

"You can count on me, Fitzpatrick," Uncle Mark said heartily. "I never wanted her to come in the first place. Well, all's well that ends well." He stroked his mustache, well pleased.

At Uncle Mark's fatuous words a bolt of cold, hard rage swept over me, mixing with my shame and mortification. I threw back my shoulders, tossed my still damp hair back, and met Evan's unreadable eyes with a brilliant, cheerful gaze.

"You tricky little thing," Uncle Mark chided me with a misguided attempt at playfulness. "It looks like your brief sojourn as a spy is over. You never let on that Fitzpatrick here was keeping an eye on you. I would have felt a lot easier about the whole thing. Evan's one of Lord Bateman's top men."

"Oh, he's very, very good," I said brightly in a high clear voice. "I had no idea, uncle, that he was working for Bones. You know how gullible I can be; I thought he had conceived a grand passion for me and that was why he was following me around Venice. Isn't that absurd?" If my brittle voice was close to tears Uncle Mark was too obtuse to notice.

"Well, well, when all's said and done, Evan's a very clever fellow," he remarked cheerfully. "And I'm sure you're delighted that he was just doing his job. You've never had any interest in young men; though damn me, it's about time you did. Well, we'll get you back to England and see what we can do about it. Wouldn't want her to end up on the shelf, would we?" he questioned Evan jovially, and I nearly screamed.

"Well, I've had a fascinating time," I said brightly, quick to change the subject. "But I'm quite exhausted. I think I'd like a bath, Maggie, and a rest, if we're to catch the train this evening." Turning my back on the three of them, I started off in the direction of the kitchen. The tears were beginning to come, and I wanted to be well out of the way as quickly as possible.

I paused by the door, counting on the dimness to shield my tear-streaked face from Evan's cold, prying, spying, damnable eyes. "Good-bye, Mr. Fitzpatrick. It's been most instructive." And before he had a chance to reply, if he even wanted to, I turned and continued with deliberate and unhurried grace into the kitchen, closing the door behind me with a soft click.

Maggie wasn't far behind me. One look at my stony, tear-streaked face, however, and she kept all her questions to herself. "It won't take long to get the bath ready, Miss Lucy. The gentlemen have left the house for a bit; you could go on up to your room."

"I'll bathe here," I said numbly, dragging the huge iron washtub into the middle of the room.

"Do you want to talk about it?" she questioned in a low voice.

"No, Maggie. Not now, and maybe not ever." And coldly, grimly, I turned my face away from her sympathy, lest I give way completely.

I have always detested self-pity, but oh, my God, I did feel so damnably sorry for myself. I sat in the tub and soaked away the stains and traces of the last twenty-four hours and knew I had only myself to blame for it all. Only my absurd complacence that had me ready to believe a man like Evan Fitzpatrick would fall in love at first sight simply because I did. If I had left him alone he would have watched me from a distance, protecting me from Holger's brigands and leaving my pathetic virginity intact.

But no, I had had to chase, and flirt, and tease, and finally invite him into my bed, all under the mistaken notion that he had developed a grand passion for me and was too shy and cynical to do anything about it.

Shy! He was about as shy as an adder. And as honest and straightforward. Why hadn't he simply told me? I had certainly given him chances enough. All he'd had to do was look at me out of those aloof, beautiful silver-blue eyes and say, "Child, I am not following you for any reason other than espionage." But he'd allowed me to trick myself—no, even encouraged it.

"You're getting the floor wet with all that splashing," Maggie said dryly. "And I won't have time to wash it before we catch the train, what with all the packing I have to do."

"Then it can mold and mildew with my blessings," I said bitterly. "And this whole house can tumble into the lagoon for all I care."

"Miss Lucy," Maggie said gently.

"Don't call me that!" I cried, splashing some more. "My name is Luciana. If some idiot of an English spy can't get my name straight that doesn't mean you have to forget after twenty-three years."

"I wish you wouldn't carry on so," she continued. "It's not as black as you think. He does care for you, I'm sure he does. How could he help it?"

I took a deep, shuddering breath and met her troubled gaze with a weak semblance of a smile. "No, he doesn't care for me, Maggie. The sooner I accept that, the better. I suppose I'd better go home and marry Johnny Phillips after all." I rose, dripping from the tub, and caught the thick, clean towel she held for me. "And we'll simply have to hope our first child isn't as premature as Mama's."

"Well," she shrugged, "with any luck you won't have to worry about such things. I've finished with your yellow dress, Miss Lucy . . . Luciana, and you can wear that. You'll look a treat, I know you will."

I didn't feel beautiful. I stared at my reflection and saw a cold, sad, mournful face. No longer a Giorgione Madonna, but a Renaissance Magdalene instead. With only myself to blame for it.

My nose wrinkled in sudden distaste. There was a familiar, rather foul odor emanating from somewhere in the room. Staring around me, my eyes fell on something I'd missed before. A gaily wrapped package on my bed.

Tearing off the wrappings, I discovered a bottle of the nasty lilac scent Tonetti used so liberally about his person. There was no sign of a note anywhere around it, and with misgivings I unstoppered the filthy stuff. The bottle was empty except for the overwhelming traces of scent and a squashed-up note.

I spent a few futile minutes trying to dislodge the missive before smashing the bottle on the marble floor. The note this time was short and terse, unlike Tonetti's usual style. The spelling, however, was just as atrocious.

"Dear Lady," it read. "I am hiding in the Palazzo Carboni. The Tedeschi have followed me here and are watching all the time. Of your goodness, please to come and rescue me and the paper. If you take the paper I will manage to escape myself. Deliver the paper to Signore Evan Fitzpatrick. Yours in dire need, Enrico Tonetti."

In a moment my mind was made up. I had spent far too much valuable time mooning after the so-clever Mr. Fitzpatrick. If I were to tell him and Uncle Mark of Tonetti's predicament I had no doubt they would try to storm the place. A single woman had a much better chance of success, and I was that lone woman.

A knock sounded on my door, and I thanked heaven I had shoved the small, straight chair in front of it.

"It's only me, Miss Lucy," Maggie called. "Mr. Fitzpatrick asked if he might see you in private before he has to leave."

I bit my lip to stifle the protest. "Where is he going?" I asked casually.

"He's got to talk with the Austrian authorities before you can be allowed to leave Venice. He seems most disturbed, Miss Lucy. You really ought to see him." Her voice was wheedling, and my resolve stiffened.

"I don't think so, Maggie. Tell him I'm resting, and that I asked you to say good-bye." I kept my voice languid as I pinned up my still-damp hair with hasty fingers.

"I don't think he'll like that, miss."

"I don't give a damn," I said in the same sweet voice as I tied my best bonnet on, grabbed a pair of gloves, and headed for the balcony. "If he ever comes to England I will see him there. By the way, Maggie, who brought the package?"

"That nasty-smelling box? A very dirty little boy. He said it was from his father. What have you been doing while you've been in Venice, Miss Lucy?"

"Nothing, Maggie, nothing at all."

A loud, irritated sigh came from the other side of the door. "All right, Miss Lucy. You take a nap and we'll be ready to go in a few short hours."

"Fine," I yawned. And, tensing my muscles, I dropped over the balcony and onto the pavement five feet below.

CHAPTER SEVENTEEN

The Palazzo Carboni was not at all difficult to find. Uncle Mark had pointed it out to us on our first trip down the Grand Canal as an example of the foolishness of Venetians. A very rich Venetian noble had begun the grandiose structure, only to run out of funds by the time the first floor was completed. Despite the architect's screams of despair, a second, shorter story was added, giving the poor building an absurdly pinheaded appearance. It had been lived in by various families until it reached its present state of dereliction, the home, like some of the other great palazzos during this time of *dimostrazióne*, of rats and the large Venetian alley cats. When I thought of poor, fastidious Tonetti living in those dank cellars my heart went out to him.

The palazzo, for obvious reasons, was uncomfortably close to the barracks. Tonetti hadn't gotten far last night, I thought unhappily, pulling my large, shielding bonnet closer around my face. I was counting on the light of day, the demureness of my dress, and the large, unflattering bonnet to protect me from the suspicions of any prowling Tedeschi. As I strolled along the fondaménto I barely received my share of curious glances, and it took only a moment's inattention on the patrols' part to enable me to slip into the damp, deserted hallways of what had once been intended to be the showplace of Venice.

"Tonetti!" I whispered loudly, stepping gingerly over the littered passageway. "Where are you?" A dark, eerie silence answered me, and a rat scuttled across my foot.

Barely suppressing a scream, I turned to run out the way I had come. And then I remembered Evan Fitzpatrick, those cold, silver-blue eyes telling me I had outlived my usefulness in Venice, and my resolve stiffened. Gritting my teeth, I turned once more to those long, empty hallways with their lofty proportions and their sleeping bats, the cobwebs and filthy litter degrading the noble lines of the building. On silent feet I moved along, every now and then calling Tonetti's name in a loud whisper, with no answer but the scuffle of tiny paws.

I was almost finished with my swift, silent tour of the ground floor when another small, strange noise alerted me to the fact that I was not alone. I could feel the tiny hairs on the back of my neck rise, and I turned around with all the grace and calm I could muster to face Holger von Wolfram's small, glittering, piglike eyes.

"Are you looking for something, Fräulein del Zaglia? Or should I say, looking for someone?"

I let out a silly little laugh. "Why, Colonel von Wolfram, fancy meeting you here of all places! I was just taking a tour of the old palazzo. My parents had told me of it when I was a child, and I've always taken a great interest in architecture. I thought before I left . . ."

"I am sure you have. The barracks that are nearby, for instance, I'm sure must have proved fascinating to a scholarly young lady like yourself."

"The barracks?" I echoed vaguely. "I don't believe I've seen them. Are they fairly ancient?"

"Old enough. You will be far more enthralled with the new prisons. They were built in the sixteenth century, but I think you might prefer them to the older ones."

"I don't think I'd care to see the prisons, thank you," I said with icy dignity.

"No?" he said politely. "Well, I doubt if you'll have much choice in the matter. Why do you suppose we allowed Tonetti's note to reach you? By arriving here you have incriminated yourself, Fräulein. As soon as we locate Tonetti and the very valuable document you stole from General Eisenhopf, there will be no question as to your guilt. I can deal with you through proper channels since my less-accepted methods didn't seem to work. I must congratulate you, Fräulein. There are not many women who could outwit the Ferrari brothers. Though I gather you had some assistance from Herr Fitzpatrick." He admired his highly polished nails. "Now if you will just tell me where Tonetti is, we can bring this entire thing to a pleasant conclusion. And do not worry, Fräulein. Hanging is a swift death, if the hangman knows his business. And our executioners are very knowledgeable."

"From lots of practice, no doubt," I snapped, my mind rushing ahead of him. Despite his interception of Tonetti's note, he obviously didn't know where he was right now. And actually, neither did I. There was no telling whether or not he'd been able to escape from this moldering wreck. Surreptitiously I slipped my reticule, which was heavily weighted with gold coins, from my wrist. "And what if I prefer not to die, Colonel?" I said conversationally. "When Venice is ceded to France I doubt they'd countenance the murder of a woman."

"You are forgetting the revolution," he said grimly. "A great many women lost their heads, some even as pretty as you, my dear. But once we regain the very important piece of paper Venice will never be returned to France," he smirked. "So you see . . ." The reticule hit him with full force, the weight of it knocking him off balance.

I didn't hesitate a second. I was off at a run before the purse left my hand, down the long, littered corridors, leaping over trash and garbage and cats, my heart about to burst, my lungs aching, running, running, running, with Holger's booted feet closer and closer behind me.

"It is useless, Fräulein," he shouted, tripping on a large black cat who proceeded to spit at him, "my men are waiting outside. You will never escape!"

I didn't waste my time answering his lies. I just kept running. For a moment it looked as if I might win, that Holger was so far behind me he'd never catch up. And then a large, evil-looking rodent ran in front of me, catching at my skirts, and I fell amid all the ruin, rolling over the disgusting rat and ending in a huddle by the dark, wet corner.

Before I had time to gather my dazed wits about me Holger was there, leaning over me with a grin of vile proportions, a hundred teeth seeming to shine in the dimly lit corridor.

"I will find Tonetti, never fear," he said, panting

and disheveled. "But first I will take care of you, Fräulein." Two meaty hands fastened around my throat and began pressing. The dark corridor became even darker, with tiny bursts of light in the back of my brain. "I will take the pleasure of finishing you myself. This"—and the hands tightened—"is for the trouble you have caused me. And this"—even tighter—"is for your damnable father who made a fool out of me. And this"—and the voice seemed to come from a long ways away—"is for your lovely mother."

And then suddenly the pressure was gone, and I collapsed back into the corner, gasping for breath, the pain in my throat so horrid I thought I would prefer to die. As I lay there trying to pull myself together I could hear the sounds of a desperate fight, and the scent of overblown lilacs assailed my nostrils.

"Are you all right, dear lady?" Tonetti's voice came from somewhere near, and two soft hands began patting mine ineffectually. I struggled into a sitting position, my eyes trying to focus on the two men struggling. "Where were you?" I tried to demand, but my voice came out in a hoarse croak.

"I was watching all the time," he announced proudly. "Thank heaven Signore Fitzpatrick arrived in time. I thought you were done for."

A horrid, rattling sigh suddenly issued forth from the enmeshed fighters, and one figure slowly detached itself, leaving the other limp on the bloodstained floor. I looked up to meet the cold, embittered silver-blue eyes of Evan Fitzpatrick.

"He's dead," he said briefly, not bothering to look at me. "Do you have the paper?"

Tonetti jumped up, all eagerness. "Enrico Tonetti, at your service, Signore Fitzpatrick. Let me tell you what a pleasure it has been to serve you, and to render my small assistance to the lovely Madonna del Zaglia. I can only . . ."

"Do you have the paper?" The voice was cold as ice, and Tonetti stammered to a halt. Searching through the somewhat tattered gondolier's outfit he still wore, he came up with the battered blue missive.

"Signore Fitzpatrick, my money . . . ?"

"Your money will be sent to you." Evan snatched the paper out of Tonetti's nerveless hands and tucked it into his pocket after no more than a cursory glance. Such an anticlimactic disposal of all that I had worked and risked my life for was almost more than I could bear. But Evan continued smoothly, ignoring my involuntary start of protest, "Do not think, Tonetti, that I didn't notice your heroic actions today. If it had been up to you she would have died."

Such concern warmed me, but only for a moment. He reached down and yanked me to my feet with such force I fell against him. He righted me instantly, and the rage on his handsome face was so formidable that I quailed.

Holger's armed guards were, as I had guessed, a fabrication. We left the palazzo with no difficulty, Tonetti's sad, dark eyes following us speculatively. I wished I could say good-bye to him, but I didn't dare with the gimlet-eyed brute beside me.

Not a word did he speak to me during the gondola ride down the Grand Canal, not a glance did he give me. It was as if I were beneath his contempt. I sat there, huddled and miserable, my throat aching, wondering what I could say to him, not daring to say a word.

We were just pulling up to the railroad station when he spoke, and his words were like tiny daggers sinking into my flesh. "Ferland and your maid are waiting for you," he said coldly. "You'd best hurry."

"Evan . . ." I tried to speak, but the noise that came out of my damaged throat was barely recognizable.

No sympathy crossed his furious face. "With any luck you'll never talk again," he said in a low, bitter voice. "And if we had more time I'd beat you within an inch of your life for running off like that. Of all the wicked, stupid things. . . !"

He jumped out of the docked gondola and pulled me onto the fondaménto, his hands rough and painful. "We're only lucky someone didn't die because of your willful stupidity. Go back to England, Lucy."

And with that he turned and left me, striding off down the quay without a backward glance for the poor, lovesick, angry girl he left behind.

"Where the hell have you been?" Uncle Mark exploded from directly behind me. "We've looked everywhere for you! Fitzpatrick took off like a bat out of hell when he read that message you left in your room. I somehow don't think you've been very straightforward with me, my girl." He peered at me more closely, something in my face breaking through his outrage. "Are you all right?" he asked gently.

"Perfectly fine," I croaked, placing a shielding hand against my aching throat. "Mr. Fitzpatrick just dropped me off. We had a small contretemps, but everything is just fine."

"What in God's name happened to you, Lucy?" he demanded, and I winced at the appellation.

"Holger von Wolfram tried to kill me," I replied briefly. "I'll tell you all about it once we leave Venice. Shall we go?"

The Demon Count's Daughter

"I suppose Fitzpatrick saved you," he speculated. "It's a lucky thing he got you here in time. It would have been no more than you deserved if we'd gone off without you. You'd have had to rely on Fitzpatrick's good graces, and he never was much the one for the ladies. Of a certain type, that is."

"Well, you've saved him from a fate worse than death," I croaked. "Shall we go?" I repeated, wanting to stay, wanting him to leave me behind, some rash, romantic part of me wanting to run back to the apartment by La Fenice and throw myself at Evan's feet.

"I suppose we'd better. I don't think he really would have minded, you know," he added enigmatically as he handed me into the private coach and the furious recriminations of Maggie.

"Who?" I asked, wearied at Uncle Mark's irritating habit of harking back to ancient conversations. "Who wouldn't have minded what?"

"I don't think Evan Fitzpatrick would have minded having you left on his doorstep," Uncle chuckled.

"Well, we'll never know, will we?" I said bitterly.

"You can ask him when he comes to England."

"He never comes to England. He prefers to

abandon his son to his brother and run around Europe playing spy."

Uncle Mark looked unconvinced. "Well, I wouldn't be surprised if he found an excuse in the very near future to arrive in Somerset. Thanks to you and Tonetti he won't be needed in Venice much longer. As a matter of fact I'll wager you ten pounds that he does."

"And I'll lay you a fiver," Maggie piped up.

I looked at the two of them through tear-filled eyes, both of them so very dear to me. The train started with a jerk, and we pulled slowly out of the Venice station. "You are both trying to cheer me up," I said damply. "And I appreciate it. And I'll also take your money, and double you!"

CHAPTER EIGHTEEN

"Luciana, my dove, would you do me a favor?" My lovely, small, delicate mother interrupted my thoughts as I sat disconsolately on the terrace, staring out over the rolling hills of Somerset. "Your brother Paolo's little friend has disappeared. He's quite unhappy, and I wondered if you might be persuaded to look for him."

Belatedly I roused myself from my torpor. I had been very lucky indeed to have suffered no more than a gentle scold from Mama and not a word of reproach from my father. One look at my stricken face when we arrived back in England had silenced my parents' natural rage, and during the last two weeks I had been both cosseted and blessedly left alone, to get over my broken heart as best I could. I had no doubt Maggie and Uncle Mark had filled them in on all the gruesome details of our sojourn in Venice, down to my night spent on Durano in the company of Evan Fitzpatrick, but apart from a few more reassuring hugs than normal, my parents behaved as if nothing had happened. I couldn't have been more grateful.

"Which one?" I questioned idly. The hot English sun added to my lassitude, draining me of my usual energy, so that all I had done for the past two weeks was sit on the terrace and stare off into the distance.

"Oh, you haven't met this one yet. Paolo's been off visiting with his people, and the two of them arrived last night after you'd retired," Mama said blithely, a surprisingly mischievous expression in her china-blue eyes. "The boy is quite lonely and unhappy, and apparently wandered off while Paolo was talking with his brothers."

"Well, Paolo's brothers can be a bit overwhelming," I said caustically. There were five of them, ranging from my oldest brother, Lucifero, who was twenty-four and surprisingly sedate, down to Marco, age one and a half, who was already horrifyingly demonic. Paolo, at age ten, was right in between and had friends wandering in and out so frequently I barely noticed them among our massive brood.

"But you will be a dear and go look for him, won't you?" she entreated, knowing full well that I would. "You are so good with children."

"You mean you're tired of me moping around

all the time?" I said, and Mama smiled her charming smile.

"That, too, darling. A walk will do you good before lunch."

As I strolled aimlessly across the lawns I thought back to that curiously naughty expression on my mother's pretty face. She had never been terribly adept in the art of prevarication, and briefly I wondered what was going on in her active mind. Before I had time to work it out, however, I came to my favorite old oak tree, my ancient refuge from a hoard of brothers, all eager to tease me about my height or pull my long, black hair.

Tilting back my head, I looked up in the leafy branches and immediately espied a small figure perched halfway up.

"Hallooo," I said in a soft, friendly voice so as not to frighten him. "What are you doing in my tree?"

"Is this your tree?" A young voice floated down, and I could hear the traces of tears in it. "I'll come down."

"Oh, no, don't bother," I waved him back. "Do you mind if I come up?"

A disbelieving laugh floated down. "Ladies can't climb trees," he scoffed.

"This one can," I replied, plopping down on the

grass and stripping off my shoes and stockings. I rolled up my sleeves, tucked my voluminous skirts into my waistband, exposing an indecent amount of calf and ankle and snowy white pantalets, and began the climb.

By the time I reached the boy I was more than slightly out of breath, but game as ever. For the first time since I had left Venice I felt a small trace of happiness. And then I looked at the boy, and my triumph faded.

"My, that was splendid," he said with great enthusiasm, his silver-blue eyes meeting mine and his young mouth curving into a grin. "I didn't think anyone your age could do that."

Quickly I put a rein on my emotions. "Oh, I'm not so very old," I said casually. "And I bet both my mother and father could climb up here even faster than I did."

"I like your mother," he confided. "I don't have one anymore, and I didn't like her very much when I did. But yours seems just the sort of mother one should have."

"And what do you think of my father?"

"He's a little frightening at first, but I think he doesn't really mean it. He seems like a pretty good father, too, but I like mine better."

"You still have a father then?" I questioned artlessly, holding my breath for his answer.

The shadow came down over his plain, earnest young face. "Yes, I do. And he's the best man in the world, and it's not his fault that he can't be with me right now."

"I'm sure it's not," I soothed him.

"Sooner or later he'll come for me, and we can go back to Penstow. That's our house in Cornwall. It's by the sea, and it's very beautiful and very old. It's made of stone, and the roof leaks a little, but we have a barn with cows and baby kittens, and houses for the men who work there, and a beach to swim from."

"You're very homesick, aren't you?" I questioned gently.

He nodded his bright gold curls, and I wanted to press his little head against me. Instead I gripped the thick branch tightly and swung my legs in an aimless fashion.

"It's all right with Uncle Simon and Aunt Sophie," he continued stoutly. "They live in Somerset, too, you know. But it's not the same as having your very own father, is it?"

"No, it's not the same," I agreed quietly. "Listen, Jamie . . . your name is Jamie, isn't it?" He nodded; and I felt a queer little feeling rush through me. Not that I had needed that last confirmation; the eyes had been proof enough. "There's nothing we can do about your father. He's off in Venice, and we can't make him come and get you any sooner than he wants to. But why don't you and I just spend the day out here, away from the house and all those people. Paolo's a very good sort of fellow, but he hasn't seen his brothers in a long time, and they get awfully rowdy. I know of an excellent fishing hole . . . you do like to fish, don't you?"

"Rather," he exclaimed, his eyes lighting up. "I used to go fishing with my father, after my mother left. But ladies don't fish."

"And ladies don't climb trees, or go barefoot," I mimicked. "I don't know where you've gotten your ideas about ladies, Jamie, me lad, but this lady does all those things and more. Are you game?"

A big grin split his face. "I bet I catch more fish than you."

"You're on." I paused. "By the way," I said deliberately, words that I never thought I'd say. "My name is Lucy."

It was a lovely day. I cajoled some simple fishing tackle out of Muggs, one of our tenant farmers, and very tactfully allowed Jamie to catch two more fish than I did. We threw them all back but had great fun wading in the brook, splashing each other and shrieking with inordinate merriment. I showed him my secret cave and the ancient raven's nest that had long since been deserted. We wandered through my favorite blackberry patch and ate so much we felt sick. My hair came unpinned as always and tangled down my back, my arms were scratched from the blackberry bushes, and my dress was ripped in a dozen places.

Jamie looked a trifle better, but then, he was dressed for an excursion in the woods. Even so, it was an odd pair of ragamuffins that made their way across the lawn in the late afternoon sunset, and I wondered a trifle guiltily whether anyone had gotten the wind up after our long disappearance. We had just reached the steps when Maddelena appeared, jabbering noisily in Italian and throwing up her hands in excitement.

"You'd better go with her," I advised Jamie, who looked uneasy at the sight of Maddelena's witchlike appearance. "She wants to clean you up." I gave him an encouraging little nudge, and he followed her dutifully enough. The sight of his small, compact little body and the soft nape of his neck beneath the gold curls made me want to snatch him back from my old nurse and hug him fiercely. I controlled the impulse, but just barely.

"You're wanted on the terrace, Miss Lucy," Maggie popped out of the door, bustling with excitement. "Best hurry up and change."

"If I'm wanted they'll have to take me as I

am," I said calmly, wiggling my toes in the long grass. "Can you have someone go down to the giant oak tree and get my shoes, Maggie? I'm afraid I left them there."

"Certainly, Miss Lucy. And you owe me ten pounds." She whisked herself back into the house, and I stared after her in perplexity. Mentally shrugging, I wandered around to the terrace, taking my time about it. I could see my parents' backs, my mother's with her small waist, my father tall and lean and elegant still. And then, just as they turned and saw me, I remembered what Maggie had said. And with a horrid sinking feeling I looked across the terrace and my eyes met the silver-blue gaze of Jamie's father.

"Ah, there she is at last," my father said silkily. "One thing I've always admired about my only daughter is her elegance in matters of dress. Tell me, my dear, are you always dressed with such a nicety, or are these your company clothes?"

And the one thing I've always hated about my father is his nasty, sarcastic tongue.

"Luc," my mother reproved him softly. "Don't be wicked." She turned to me, and the mischievous look was out in full force. "Luciana, darling, Jamie's father has come to fetch him. Did you find him in the woods?"

"Yes." My voice came out in a strangled croak, and I could hear my father's damnable laugh.

"Come, Carlotta." He held out an elegant arm, and my mother took it, giving him her usual adoring smile, a smile he returned, before raising a satanic eyebrow at his erring daughter. "We will leave these two alone to make their own mistakes. Don't be stubborn, child," he warned, and the two of them glided into the house before I could open my mouth to protest.

As they went I heard my mother's soft, clear voice say to Luc, . . . "I think we should go back to Edentide, my love. The Austrians will be gone soon, and I have a longing for the old place. It still seems to work its magic on people." She sighed happily.

"Whatever you say, little one. Though I think we make our own magic. . . ."

Evan stared at me for a long moment. "You look very fierce."

"Do I?"

"You shouldn't blame me, you know."

"I don't blame you for anything. Except for not telling me the truth," I accused him bitterly.

"Lucy, when you willfully involved yourself in the dangerous game of spying, you gave up any right to, or acquaintance with, honesty. It's not a truthful profession, and you should have damned well known it."

"I know it now." If this sounded sulky I couldn't help it.

He moved closer with that pantherish grace I had tried so hard to forget, and the night on Durano came rushing back to my senses with stunning force. "Do you realize," he said softly, "how silly you're being? With that dignified manner and your appearance? Your dress is torn, your bare feet are muddy, you've got freckles across your nose, and blackberry stains on your mouth. I wonder . . ."

Before I could guess his intention he had pulled me into his arms and his mouth was on mine, draining any attempt at resistance I might have shown. He raised his head and looked down at me with teasing laughter in his sunlit eyes. "You do taste of blackberries." And then he kissed me again.

"Father!" A shrill voice sounded from inside the house, and thankfully I felt myself put to one side as a small dynamo came hurtling through the French doors and into Evan's arms. As I watched father and son greet each other an uncomfortable knot formed in my throat, so that I had to swallow a few times and blink back tears.

"Have you met Lucy?" Jamie demanded when

the initial welcome was past. "I've just met her, but she's my dearest friend. I want her to come to Penstow and visit sometime. Are we going to Penstow, Father? How long can you stay this time? Isn't Lucy pretty? Do I have to go back to Uncle Simon's? Couldn't you possibly stay a bit longer this time?" The small face was wistful.

Evan laughed, his eyes lighting up his dark, scarred face and making him look almost carefree. "Yes, I've met Lucy. Yes, she's very pretty. Yes, we're going to Penstow, yes, I'm staying a long, long time. And no, you don't have to go back to Uncle Simon's."

"I don't?" he shrieked, his face suffused with joy. "Not ever? Are you going to stay with me forever and ever?"

He smiled. "Forever and ever. So, for that matter, is Lucy."

"What?" It was my turn to shriek in disbelief, only to have Jamie's strong, little arms crush the general area of my knees. "I most certainly am not!" I was torn between tears and laughter. "You don't want me at all. It was I who seduced you, and now you feel you have to be a gentleman."

"Don't be absurd. I've never behaved like a gentleman toward you, and I'm certainly not about to start."

"But you don't love me!" I wailed.

"You foolish woman, I loved you from the moment you fell at my feet in the Merceria. Or maybe it was when you went swimming in those tiny scraps of clothing in the broad daylight. It was definitely by the time you tossed the tea tray on General Eisenhopf's mistress."

"That was General Eisenhopf's mistress?" I questioned, momentarily diverted. "How nice."

"They didn't think so," he grinned. "Are you coming with us?"

"No."

"Lucy"—and his tone of voice was low and dangerous—"I am too old for all these romantic misunderstandings. If you are too stubborn I'm sure I can persuade your father to help me club you on the head and carry you off to Cornwall. You are alarmingly easy to kidnap."

"You wouldn't!"

"I would, and he would."

I had no doubt of it. Much as the idea appealed to me, it might have its share of discomfort. I looked down at the child clinging to me like a limpet and met those trusting, silver-blue eyes, so like his father's. He smiled up at me and I smiled back.

"Father," Jamie said confidently, detaching his crushing grip, "she'll come. But you have to be nicer to her if you want her to be my new mother.

You practice," he ordered his formidable father, "and I'll say good-bye to Paolo."

He disappeared into the house, past the amused and curious figures of my eavesdropping parents, and Evan turned back to me with a dangerously tender expression on his tired, scarred, handsome face. "Very wise, is my young son." And proceeded to obey Jamie's instructions. And not much practice was needed at all.

INTRODUCING...

The Romance Magazine For The 1980's

Each exciting issue contains a full-length romance novel — the kind of first-love story we all dream about...

PLUS

other wonderful features such as a travelogue to the world's most romantic spots, advice about your romantic problems, a quiz to find the ideal mate for you and much, much more.

ROMANTIQUE: A complete novel of romance, plus a whole world of romantic features.

ROMANTIQUE: Wherever magazines are sold. Or write Romantique Magazine, Dept. C-1, 41 East 42nd Street, New York, N.Y. 10017

INTERNATIONALLY DISTRIBUTED BY DELL DISTRIBUTING, INC.